BOOKS BY

STONE COLD JOE

T he old marshal of Snake Pit, Texas, knew that they would kill him. He had had to kill Turk's baby brother and Turk would be bringing his Cloudy Hills gang of gunslingers, murderers and cutthroats here to avenge that death. Joe couldn't run away and had no friends to help him but, tough as they were, Joe would see that some of Turk's gang preceded him into the afterlife.

TALKING FIRE HAND

C harlie took a slow breath raising one eyebrow in question, trying to give the man every opportunity to rethink his actions and surrender. He didn't want to risk speaking and alerting the other two that his back was to them. They might just try to put a bullet in it.

The black-haired man didn't stop and, as the outlaw's gun came level pointing at him, Charlie pulled the trigger and through the gun smoke saw the man disappear as he was hit with the buckshot.

A shorter, personal version of 'Talking Fire Hand'
was published under the title of
Charlie: the Family Edition

TALKING FIRE HAND

Stephen C. Porter

Order this book online at www.trafford.com
or email orders@trafford.com

Most Trafford titles are also available at major online book retailers.

Printed in the United States of America.

ISBN: 978-1-4269-3634-0 (sc)

ISBN: 978-1-4269-3635-7 (hc)

ISBN: 978-1-4269-3665-4 (e-book)

Library of Congress Control Number: 2010908701

*Our mission is to efficiently provide the world's finest, most comprehensive book publishing
service, enabling every author to experience success. To find out how to publish your
book, your way, and have it available worldwide, visit us online at www.trafford.com*

Trafford rev. 6/25/2010

 www.trafford.com

North America & international
toll-free: 1 888 232 4444 (USA & Canada)
phone: 250 383 6864 ♦ fax: 812 355 4082

CHAPTER 1

The day was as still as death and death was what was out there. Charlie listened with the ear of an experienced hunter. As he listened, he calmly rolled a pebble with his fingers. It helped him to think and kept his fingers and hands limber for what he had to do.

There were three of them and they had him surrounded. It was a game that he had played many times. They thought that they had him cornered but Charlie was right where he wanted to be and they were right where Charlie wanted them.

One was just a little left of center, behind an old ant hill. He thought that he was well hidden but when he shifted his position a little while ago, he had created a slight dust cloud that could be seen by an experienced tracker for 300 yards.

Charlie could easily shoot through the hill with his Sharps 50 but he did not want to alert the other two just yet.

One was slowly working his way in closer on Charlie's right side.

"He wasn't doing too bad." thought Charlie. He was coming in through some tall grass and was only moving it once in a while and he was making no sound. He would be ready to kill in a few minutes if he kept coming like that.

It was the third man that was setting the pace for the kill here. He was behind Charlie and was coming up the wash that Charlie knew ended 30 feet behind him. It was very steep the last 10 feet and that man would not be able to peek over before exposing himself.

Looking out over the almost flat countryside, Charlie glanced at the swaying prairie grass and gently rolling landscape, broken occasionally by the small clusters of poplar trees that always seem to spring up and thrive wherever their seed finds enough shelter to keep the trees alive enough to flourish in the constant west wind. Charlie had fallen into a little depression almost at the top of one of those rolls in the land and he had a good vision field of the three men that were trying to kill him.

The sun was halfway up in the eastern sky, shining down on Charlie's back and he could feel the sweat, that it's heat was creating, as it slide down his spine and around his hips. His blue eyes never wavered as the sweat also ran down his straight, angular nose and dropped off the end of it.

It was almost time and Charlie laid his Sharps on the ground in front of him in the general direction of mister "ant hill". Mister "hidden in the grass" was going to be a little late so Charlie decided that he would have to kill him on the fly as he ran away.

Rolling over, he pointed his 12 gauge, double barreled shotgun at the wash where he knew that man must come up and waited. The sun shone down the barrel at him but was hidden from the other two by the outside lip of the depression.

Charlie could hear him now as he loosened dirt just before the last assent. Two hairy dirty hands appeared, one clawed at the edge of the wash while the other held a cocked dragoon .45 pistol that he dug the butt into the dirt to hold him from falling back down into the wash. The man's dirty black hat appeared next followed by thick long black hair. His heavy eyebrows were set above eyes that were too close together and a long hawk nose, short upper lip and pinched mouth, giving him a tight evil look. He was concentrating on getting his balance on the edge of the wash and did not notice Charlie but, when he saw the black twin barrels staring at him, realization made his eyes start to open in fear. He locked his free arm on the edge and tried to raise the .45 for a shot. Charlie took a slow breath, hesitating; trying to give the man every opportunity to rethink his actions and surrender, but, as the outlaw's gun came level pointing at Charlie, he pulled the trigger and through the gun smoke saw the man disappear as he was hit with the buckshot.

Quickly rolling over, Charlie was just in time to see "in the grass" with his head above the grass trying to see what was happening. He had the same black hair and pinched features but looked younger and his mouth hung open thoughtlessly like. He had been good at moving through the grass but had forgotten about the danger and was chest high above the grass trying to see; his rifle moving back and forth seeking to find and take Charlie's life. Charlie gave him the second barrel of the shot gun and watched the buckshot mow the top of the grass down as it hit the man. A red stain appeared on his chest as he was thrown backwards into the grass.

Putting the gun down, Charlie grasped the Sharps and sighted along its long barrel, just about 8 inches above the ground and about where a man would lie behind the ant hill. Without a hesitation, Charlie squeezed of his shot. There was not a sound from the ant hill after the bullet puffed up dust as it went through the hill and into whatever was behind it.

Charlie knew that he had made his kills but he was also a cautious man and he was in no hurry. He took a sip of water and watched the countryside around him as he broke open the shotgun and put two more shells in the double chambers. The Sharps was next, pulling back the hammer and flipping the shell out, Charlie slid another, almost 5 inch long, shell down the open hole.

"You never can tell what that noise might bring" he thought.

It also gave him time to think back to how this situation started. As Charlie thought, he reloaded his guns. The shotgun was a gift from his father for his 16th. birthday. Even though it had a walnut, hand carved stock and an extra long barrel, it was all business when

3

it came to shooting true and fast. It was a double barreled gun but the barrels were one over the other in rifle fashion, called an over/under double-barreled. Also, the maker had softened a thick piece of bull-hide and attached it to the shoulder mount so that the gun had less recoil when it was fired. He had also put in two little metal kickers that, when the gun was broke open to load, kicked the spent shells out so all a man had to do was put two more shells in and close it and he was ready to go again. It only had one trigger and one hammer so, when it was cocked, you could get one shot for each time you squeezed the trigger or hold the trigger and both shots would come almost together. The bottom barrel was slightly longer than the top so the hammer hit it first and, if the trigger was not pulled, stopped. When the trigger was squeezed the second time the second spring and lever released to let the hammer travel on to the second barrel.

It was a beautiful working gun; well balanced, easy and, being a 12 gauge, powerful enough to stop a mad bull, as long as you were using slugs. Using double-o buckshot would cut a man in two at 30 yards.

The Sharps had come from the North Country; Canada probably. It had a white maple stock which made it softer than an oak stock and flexible enough to take a hard go and stay true. Someone had also rifled the barrel; a real pro because the gun shot true to within a half an inch at five hundred yards. Charlie had never seen another gun as accurate as this one was. It had been reworked from a cap and ball system to a British .50 caliber center-fire cartridge. The hammer had been moved from the outside to the inside center behind the barrel so, when the hammer was cocked, a man could slide the cartridge into the barrel. Firing the rifle brought the hammer up and into the cartridge center. Cocking the gun again took the hammer out of the way and, because it was a center fire, the spent shell could easily be pulled from the barrel and another one put in.

All the time Charlie spent reloading his guns was also spent looking and listening. He now knew that all three men were dead. The little birds were searching for food right beside their hiding

4

places and were not afraid. Also the bugs had started to hum and buzz again. Nothing human moved.

Charlie looked over at his bay gelding. He was quietly eating some grass that he found tasty. They had wanted his horse alive. Not only was he a horse built for speed but he had a deep chest that spoke of great endurance. They had all but killed their horses trying to get away from Charlie and a man without a horse in this Montana country could die before he got to a settlement.

Charlie had arrived too late, where the chase started.

These three had found a farm about two weeks back. The farmer, an average middle aged man with a pretty wife and twin boys, about 7 years old, had taken them in and fed them.

They had repaid the farmer by cutting his boys' throats, gutting him and, after using his wife for their desires for about a week, had bashed her brains in with the farmers axe.

People like this turned Charlie's stomach but he hadn't intended to kill them; he had thoughts about taking them back to the law.

Charlie had been traveling west anyway and had pushed these three hard from North Dakota into Montana. They had twisted and turned through mountains and river valleys, trying to shake him but Charlie had practically grown up with the Indians and had excelled in their hide and seek games.

He was the son of the Indian missionary 'Talking Hand'; named that by the Indians because he talked from the bible that he always carried in his hand and, because he lived by it's words, he was well respected among many of the western Indian bands. His father was known around Washington by his real name, Charlie Power; Charlie was named after his father but his mom, Betty, called him Chuck so they would know who she was talking to.

The Indian Chiefs had sent Charlie with their most experienced and best warriors and hunters to train him in tracking, fighting and bow and knife handling. He had also learned many of their languages, medicines and habits. His Dad, being a determined and diligent man, had taught him how to watch, listen and learn everything that he could from as many as he could.

5

Charlie had proved to be a first rate student, not wanting to shame his teachers and it seemed to come naturally to him to be good at tracking and fighting. Charlie was a gentle, peace loving man but trouble always seemed to find him and he would do whatever he had to do to stop it.

As he tracked these three, he had watched as they grew more and more desperate and pushed their horses to exhaustion. He knew that it was just a matter of time until their horses gave out and he caught them. Few horses could keep up the pace that Charlie's bay, Joe, could set. Even now, Joe still looked as fresh as when they started after running the three murderer's horses into the ground.

This morning Charlie knew that he would catch them. Two of their horses had fallen yesterday and they had not put them out to feed where they stopped last night.

By 8 o'clock, Charlie had seen where they had left two horses, about a half of a mile apart, and had continued on foot. Charlie had skirted the horses to the north and from then on expected an ambush very soon.

He had guessed right; just past the head of this wash, he could see the third horse but not the men. He knew that they were waiting in the grass for him. While he rode up to the wash, Charlie located the three; one by one he had spotted them and marked their hiding spots.

They were going to ambush him in the open just past the wash head. He had glanced down into the wash as he rode by it and seen the climb that one of them would have to make to get behind him.

He already had his Sharps rifle in his hands and, as he came to the top of the rise, he pull his shotgun from its scabbard and dropped off the side of his horse at the same time as he heard the bullet go by his shoulder. His sharp eyes had been watching the three and had calculated correctly the time that they would open fire.

Joe, used to gunfire and bullets, had walked off to some waiting grass while Charlie had slid into a dip that he had located for his occupation. The way he left the saddle in such a hurry, they could not be sure but what they had got him and Charlie smiled and made no move to help them figure it out.

He had watched as number three had slipped down into the wash and started sneaking up behind him. Then, the rest became history real fast.

The farmer and his family he had buried and prayed over; these three would not get that luxury.

As Charlie got up, the first thing he did was settle his two colt 45 pistols in a comfortable and easy-to-get-at position. Unlike most people who wore one pistol or the ones who wore two but were only good with one at a time, Charlie could use both independently of each other at the same time; both with a very good degree of accuracy. It was not that Charlie was special, but handling guns well came naturally to him and he had accepted that fact. The speed came from lots of practice. They were tools that he kept well oiled and used for the everyday chores of getting food and playing with.

He only had these guns for a couple of months and he had bought them because they had the new single action trigger. This meant that when he squeezed the trigger, the hammer went back in a cocked position and then fired as he kept squeezing. His old navies were double actions that he had to thumb the hammer back then squeeze the trigger to fire it. These new single action guns made him just a little bit faster getting his shot away. They were also a little lighter and much more dependable; he had already started to wear a couple of smooth places on the handles from his practices.

Charlie wore his guns at a 45 degree angle, each pointing in across his middle.

Some people would laugh and say that Charlie was going to blow his privates off one of these days but they always wanted him around and on their side when the bullets started flying. Charlie's draw was just a flick of his wrists, if anyone could ever see it and his bullets always went were he wanted them to go.

It was obvious that Charlie was a gun fighter and not a gun slinger. There was a difference. A gun fighter took the time to be deadly accurate and his guns were well looked after tools. A gun slinger notched his guns for show and made his living being fast and cruel. Fair play only interfered with his income. Their accuracy was sacrificed for speed and could spray bullets over a wider field; sometimes hitting more than their intended victims.

Charlie needed no income; he had made a small fortune befriending and protecting those miners that hit pay dirt in the gold fields in his younger days and was just looking to see what life was like in different places.

Charlie's ace in the hole was a two edged stiletto style knife in a built-in seethe in his pants; sewn into his right-side seam between his hip and his knee. Because of his chaps and his guns, it was almost invisible. Blade heavy and made of the best German steel, it could be thrust like a sword, thrown or hand manipulated with equal efficiency and accuracy.

Charlie walked back and looked down into the wash. That man had fallen straight back and lay spread-eagle at the bottom. His face and upper shoulders was just a mass of flesh and bone.

As Charlie turned and walked to "in the grass", his steps were as silent as a gentle breeze. He walked on his out step. A habit he learned in Indian country. As he walked, he rolled his foot down on the very out side so there would not be a clump sound when his weight came onto it and he could shift his weight in a split second, if he felt a movable or breakable object under his boot.

"In the grass" had taken his load of buckshot in the chest and the hole was about a foot across. He still had the surprised look on his face.

Charlie continued on to "behind the ant hill" and found his work was well done. He had the same dark features as the other two but looked older than the others and more cowardly. He had not shown himself when the shooting started but left it up to his brothers to do the dangerous work; the typical characteristics of a professional back-shooter. He had taken his in the right side of his face and it had blown about a half of his skull away. The disturbed ants were already harvesting the man's flesh.

Charlie again took the time to study the surrounding countryside. An impatient man could be a dead man real fast. The Sioux claimed the territory around here but the northern Black foot tribes had been raiding here lately, too. Either tribe would welcome the chance to bring down a white man that they came across.

Satisfied, Charlie would later clean out what they had that could be used by the next poor homesteader that Charlie came across and went to help their one remaining horse.

The exhausted horse needed some water and some rest but first, Charlie walked it around slowly to keep it from stiffening up and, possibly, dieing. After a little drink, he picketed it beside Joe; his bay.

Joe was short for Joseph. The horse had been badly abused before Charlie bought him and Charlie had spent long hours talking to him and gently rubbing him down. Charlie's gentle hands and soft voice won Joseph's heart and he proved to be as loyal a horse as any Charlie had ever owned. Charlie named him Joseph for the Joseph in the Bible. He had been sold by his own, abused and hard done by but God had raised him up to be a prince. Charlie thought that suited Joe because now, after such a hard life, he was a prince of a horse.

Charlie tightened Joe's saddle cinch and, once in the saddle, cantered Joe back along the outlaw's trail. He found what he had expected. A couple of miles back he found the first down horse. It was almost dead with bloody froth bubbling out of it's nostrils at every breath it exhaled and, with a sigh; Charlie shot the horse, ending its suffering quickly. Doing what had to be done regardless of how he felt about it.

"They ran him to death" Charlie thought bitterly; then he spotted the third horse. It was a little black standing, with its head down, reins caught on some low bushes, another 1000 yards back.

As Charlie approached, the black horse lifted its head a little to look at him.

"One tough little horse" murmured Charlie and he decided that the horse would probably live. Giving it a drink with water from his canteen and poured into his hat brought an immediate improvement to the horse.

Charlie led it back to the dead animal and striping the saddle from the downed horse, adding it to the live one along with the saddle bags and bridle.

CHAPTER 2

The country here was relatively flat. A few washes cut through it, like the one that Charlie had been sheltered by. It was July and the grass and flowers were everywhere. The tallest thing around being the scrubs that had caught the horses reins. Off to the West, the direction that Charlie had been traveling in, you could just see the mountains. The air was very clear and that made it deceptive. The mountains, big as they were, looked like they were only a day or two's ride away but Charlie knew that at his present 15 to 20 miles a day riding, he wouldn't get to them for another week.

By the time Charlie arrived back at the ambush site, he knew that he was being watched. When you lived outdoors as long as he had and in as many dangerous places, you learned to heed your feelings about company. He took his time gathering up the outlaws' belongings and loaded everything onto the spare horses, he kept watching, listening and feeling and, finally locating his visitor 300 yards north. He was good. He was almost concealed behind a lone, horse sized boulder that had bushes growing all around it. He was half lying on the boulder and was laying his head sideways on it to keep his head from showing above it while he watched Charlie.

"That's an Indian trick." Charlie knew and, not being the best marksmen, also knew that he would not try a gunshot from that far away.

A Sioux would not be alone unless something out of the ordinary had happened so this might be a Black Foot scouting for a raiding party.

Charlie went about his loading as if he had seen nothing and, when he was ready, mounted Joe and started, casually away. The other two horses were surprised to find that they were free to follow as they wanted to and liking the gentleness of this man, walked along behind them.

The man watching Charlie saw a medium built man with the garb of a cowboy; the usual dusty, flannel shirt, brown pants and a tan flat-top hat. His boots were low, miners walking boots; not the usual high heeled riding boots. This gave the hint that Charlie was a very physical person and that walking was something that he was used to. The rest of Charlie's features seemed plain as could be; standing just under 6' tall, average build with brown hair and blue eyes. His face was tanned and it looked like he had a little bit of a pot belly but this belied itself. Charlie had worked hard all his life and was all muscle. His hands were thick with muscles that were as hard as rocks and his shirt hid the muscular slope of his shoulders. At 200 lbs, Charlie had been known to pick up his own weight in a box of gold and carry it 50 yards to a waiting wagon with as little effort as picking up a child.

Charlie's face held an almost constant open and honest look that could be quick to smile; which would light up his whole angular and handsome face with laughter making his eyes shine. Those same eyes could turn an icy white blue when he was angry and could seem to pierce through a person's soul looking for the offending evil.

As he rode down the first gentle slope, Charlie was busy studying the watchers position from the corner of his eye. He noticed that when he dropped into the next and much shallower wash, he would be invisible to the man for some time before he reappeared on the other side and that this wash cut back to within 100 yards of that boulder. Reaching the bottom, Charlie turned and put Joe up the wash at a faster pace. The grass deadened the sound of their traveling and, when he got to the place opposite the boulder, Charlie stood up on the saddle to look over the edge.

Sure enough, lying with his back almost to Charlie and not moving was an Indian. The low bushes around the rock hid all but his shoulders and head. Charlie went up the side of the wash with a silent rush and had covered over half of the distance to the Indian when he noticed, through the leaves, the blood stain on his back. The Indian also did not appear to have any weapons. When Charlie got to him, he found an Indian youth that had lost so much blood from a knife wound in his back that he had fallen asleep in the heat of the sun while he had watched Charlie.

Charlie quickly checked to make sure that he was breathing and then gently checked the wound. It had bled a lot but not here. It was a funny wound. It was made by a sharp knife but it looked like it was made by a badly thrown knife. It had entered the flesh at a slight angle, missing the spine and just below the ribs, and slashed across the boy's right side, ending in a vicious, open wound; almost as if the knife had fallen out itself. The back muscles had to be sewn together and stitches put in to close the wound.

While the boy was out, Charlie whistled for Joe, who came with a rush and he dug his medical kit from his saddlebags. He always carried a little something with him because he always seemed to need to heal or fix someone.

Turning to the Indian with the horses gathered around them, he decided that the boy was just the right height, on the rock, for what he had to do. Threading some fishing line through his needle, he started to sew the muscle together. The wound, he figure, had bled enough to clean it out and he didn't think he should use up anymore time before he closed the wound. It was going to bleed more anyway.

The youth groaned once and then seemed to laps into an unconscious state. Charlie worked harder. He thought "the poor kid might just be passed out or that might be the onset of death. God help him; he's too young to die now."

Sweat ran down Charlie's face and the usual drops fell from the end of his nose as he concentrated on doing a good clean job.

A half hour later, Charlie stood up from his work. The wound was sewn, bandaged and wrapped and, to Charlie's delight, the boy was still alive. "This was getting to be some interesting day." Charlie thought. He took a few minutes to study the surrounding countryside; noting the buzzards that were coming in overhead to feast on the outlaws that were not that far away. There were a half a dozen of the big birds already covering the two outlaws that Charlie could see and, he thought, probably a few more in the wash with the third one.

"Nothing like hanging out a sign and telling the world that you're here." He mussed.

Gently rolling the boy over, he held his canteen close to his lips; hoping to get some liquid into him to help replace some of the blood that he had lost. Strangely enough the boy swallowed some without waking up.

Studying his clothes, Charlie was surprised again to see that he was a Nez Pres; a southern and more easterly tribe. Montana was not were you would normally find one. They were also a very colorful and a very handsome people, living peaceably with the whites for some time now.

Absently reaching to adjust the youth's loincloth which had flapped open when Charlie rolled him over, he made another and a much more serious discovery. He was not a he but was a she. Flame red color crept up from Charlie's collar until it reached his hairline. This was a bit more than he had bargained for. She would not be an advance for a raiding party but, for sure, someone was looking for her and would not be happy to find her hurt and helpless in Charlie's care. He had to get them both away from here and into some place of shelter; well hidden from searching eyes, until she healed and Charlie learned what her story was. He had to learn and prepare for whatever dangers this situation was going to bring.

He stood up and started to earnestly study the countryside. He was looking for any thing he could use to make a travois; a one-horse cart type of affair made of two poles crossed at one end over top of the horses front shoulders, leaving the other ends to drag on the ground and tying a blanket or two across the poles in the center to hold them there, the horse could pull it along the ground and whatever was on the blankets could lie in reasonable comfort for the trip.

About a mile away, Charlie saw a stand of poplars in a mud wash. Taking Joe and after hitching the other horses to the bushes, he trotted him to the wash. As he rode nearer his keen eyesight studied the trees looking for some suitable young trees for his purpose and after selecting two green trees about 6 inches at the base, he cut them down with his hatchet and, after cutting the branches off them, cut them off again about 20' up. While he was there, he cut 6 more smaller and shorter limbs for cross pieces. Strategically placed across the travois, they could support the girl comfortably without much trouble. Dragging his bundle of tree limbs, he hurried Joe back to the girl.

All the way back he studied the countryside for signs of movement. Seeing none, he quickly built the travois; lashing the ends of the pole tops together with a part of one of the outlaws lariats. He notched the ends of the limbs before tying them to the sides of the poles; this made them fit closer and helped so they would not slide down the slopping sides of the poles. Then before he loaded the girl onto the travois, he tied a blanket across the poles and layered a few arm loads of grass over the blanket and tied another one on top of it. This made a nice comfortable mattress for her to lie on and would absorb most of the bumps.

He was careful about what he touched or exposed when he gently picked her up and laid her on the travois. Joe was the smoothest and gentlest horse, so he got to pull the travois. The tough little black horse proved to be up for a man in his saddle. Charlie decided to call him "Nails" because he seemed to be as tough as nails.

They started west again but this time Charlie put a lead rope on the third horse, a brown colored horse with grey markings on her shoulders and front legs. Joe did not need a lead rope; he kept his nose near Charlie's knee and his ears near those always gentle and often patting hands.

The travois worked wonderfully and they soon had a dozen miles between them and their meeting place. Charlie occasionally stopped to see if the girl could drink more water but all he could do was moisten her lips. Upon crossing a small stream, he carefully bathed her face, and refilled all the canteens he had. After letting the horses drink their fill, he turned upriver and walked them a mile up the stream. The alder bushes growing along the edge gave them some cover and the water would wash away their tracks.

He didn't try to hurry the horses because they needed to drink lots of water to regain their strength.

He knew that the disturbed stream bottom would send mud down stream for some time and their tracks would not be covered soon but he had seen no pursuit and was trying for a long-term fix to throw off a later tracker. Hiding a travois track was not easy.

Coming out of the water on a wide game trail, he saw a number of islands of tree growth; old buffalo wallows that had grown the ever present poplars. Heading straight for the nearest one, he circled it on the far side, went to the second and done the same thing then, while circling the third, he went into it on the opposite side to the stream.

Moving back through it so he could plainly see his back trail, he also found a slight dip; just enough to hide them if they crouched down. He quickly made camp; keeping everything below the top of the dip so it did not show to anyone outside of the tree grove. He dropped the packs close to keep the rodents and small vermin afraid to get into them and made a soft bed of leaves and moss for the girl. After rubbing the horses down he took them to the side that they had entered the grove on and picketed the two strange horses, even though Nails was getting pretty friendly. Joe he trusted completely and Charlie let him run free. He would come in an instant if he was called.

Coming back through the wallow, he stopped in the center to dig a water catch basin. Water would seep into it overnight and they could have fresh drinking water in the morning.

Charlie looked in at the girl, who was still sleeping and then made a circle just inside the tree line all the way around the tree island. He went slowly studying the country and their sanctuary, looking for anything out of the ordinary to use as a defense or weapon and looking for danger. He also collected a number of herbs and vegetables to use for medicine and food.

Glancing back just inside the edge of the trees, he saw that, except for the horses, his camp was inside the dip and could not be seen and there was a good tree cover over the dip that would disperse his campfire smoke. The older and bigger trees were in and around the dip but the tree growth spread out giving them tree cover up to 100 yards out from the dip and, with all the younger trees near the edge and mixed in through the center, gave them enough cover to be able to move around inside the tree line and still remain hidden.

Out on the prairie the grass waved in the constant breeze but was low enough to let him see even the smallest detail and for many miles in every direction. Turning, he followed the stream path through the plain. It had cut a small valley with all the spring runoffs but the tops of the alders and white birch trees along its banks showed above the grass. He knew that the water would draw every animal and human in the area to it for drinking water and shade. Many would travel along the edge of the valley, finding food on the prairie as the game trails had shown him when he left the valley.

The two other clumps of poplars were much smaller than this one and Charlie could easily see through them to the prairie on the other side.

Charlie's keen eye caught sight of a prairie chicken sitting on her nest. She was only a few feet away and was trying to be completely still hoping Charlie would not see her. Slipping his stiletto out and, with one quick step and stab, had her head off.

After completing his circle, Charlie had the chicken, 8 eggs, a half dozen herbs and about a gallon of wild vegetables. Starting a small fire, he half filled his coffee pot with water and started to cut up some vegetables and dropped them into the pot. Next he cleaned the bird, dropping the innards into the pot and staking the carcass on a stick to roast. Then he crushed a few of the herbs into the pot along with a few powders that he got from his saddlebags. Finding a can of beans in one of his added saddlebags, he pierced the top with the point of his knife and set them almost into the fire to cook.

The girl moaned and her eyes fluttered open. Her gaze, Charlie saw, was glassy and unfocused. She was running a fever.

He had laid her on a slight slope in the ground so her head was slightly above her feet. This way he could feed her and give her water without too much movement to her back wound. He had put the fire so she could easily see it, knowing that a campfire was a comfort to people in the wild. Sitting beside it, he waited to see if her eyes would focus. She needed water and food but she did not need to be scared out of her wits first.

She focused first on the fire and then on the cooking food. When her gaze went to his face, Charlie put on a small easy smile and signed "friend". He repeated this a time or two until he saw her eyes glaze a little and her body started to relax.

Taking up his canteen, Charlie knelt beside her and, after gently lifting her head, poured enough water on her lips to moisten them. She started and grabbed the canteen. Holding it to her lips she tried to gulp as much as she could. Charlie let her drink but held the canteen down so she did not get too much at one time and bloat herself. Often a dehydrated person that finally gets to water will drink too much too fast and their stomach cannot handle the sudden gush of liquid and they will throw up.

The water revived her a little and she again looked at Charlie. He again signed "friend" and, smiling a little, went back to his cooking. The smell of food was getting her attention.

While Charlie had doctored this Indian, he had studied her and now he pondered what he had learned.

Her moccasins were well worn from a lot of traveling and the front of her leggings, from the knees down, were scuffed and scratched; like she had been running in the grass a lot. Her nails were cracked and her hands were cut; also she was dirty but, upon a closer look, it was surface dirt from traveling without taking the time to wash. Her clothes were well kept and tidy. The knife wound had cut a large slash in her buckskin shirt and she was bloody from the middle of her back down to her knees and would probably have killed her if Charlie had not found her. Her long black hair was in two tight braids but was also full of leaves and dirt. She had large brown eyes and a really pretty face but she was running from something and she had a fearful and hunted look.

"Nope" Charlie said "Not a scout for a raiding party."

"But what was her story?" He thought.

While he stirred the pot and turned the bird, her eyes kept going from him to the food and back to him.

The stew was ready about the same time as the beans; the bird would be done as soon as they had eaten the vegetables, Charlie guessed.

Taking the stew and beans, he sat down beside the girl and, after pouring stew into a tin bowl and opening the bean can cover, said "Thank you, God, for this food." Then he took a spoonful of stew and blew on it until it was cool enough and held it up to the girl's mouth. She looked at him for some time then she took the stew. She swallowed it almost instantly and after that gulped food as fast as Charlie could feed her. Her strength regained so fast that she started reaching for the bowl and the spoon to feed her-self. Charlie settled in to enjoy his beans.

The bird was ready when they had eaten the stew and beans. Setting it away from the fire to cool, Charlie dug some packages out of his bags and, after mixing some of them in a cup with some dried berries rubbed it on the birds flesh. He put it into the fire, briefly, to stick the paste to the bird and then passed a leg to the girl.

As she ate, she kept looking at Charlie, the paste and the bird. Of the two she ate most of the bird. "She must have been a long time without food." Charlie thought. As they washed it down with some water, Charlie saw her eyes start to flutter and close.

"Those herbs will give her a good night's sleep." He chuckled.

The sun was setting and Charlie pulled his new "Henry" repeating rifle from its saddle scabbard. Lever action, 8 shot magazine and shiny new; it was time to try it out. The gunsmith had said that he had trued the gun up but Charlie liked to true his own guns. The Henry would not give him the power or range of the Sharps and would not give him the shorthand wallop of the shotgun but it would give him a medium gun for either short or long range, if he needed it. He had tried it a time or two and it was not bad but he liked to personalize his tools. He didn't get the chance today; all was quiet and he decided it was best left that way.

He had been traveling kind of heavy as he made his way west and had not been prepared to chase outlaws but Joe had surprised even him by carrying the weight and outlasting the outlaw's horses.

He went to tend the horses and, finding them full of grass, took them back to the stream for a drink; careful to stay on the game trail and not let them wonder after their drink. He crossed the stream, circled and at 500 yards upstream, came back across it at another game trail and circled wide, back to their tree island. All the while Charlie looked for anything that might be trouble. Scanning the skyline looking for dark spots that could be human or smoke that would tell of someone else's camp, he saw nothing. He was also careful to look closer at objects that were in plain sight. Indians would often hide half behind objects that were close to their victims knowing that the human eye will naturally look to the farthest points and overlook what is right in front of it; thinking because it is so close and has not hurt them that it must be harmless and will only focus on it if it moves.

Seeing nothing, he picketed the two spare horses, again, in a new spot and came back to the camp. The girl was still sleeping so Charlie put two more blankets on her and tucked them in to keep her warm. Next, he cut some short sticks and fashioned the frame of a lean-to over her; spreading a couple of rain slickers over the frame and adding some leafy branches to keep it from flapping. It would also help to keep the girl warmer tonight.

"Might not need it tonight" Charlie thought, "But we also might be here for awhile. Her back has to heal and it can't do that if we travel around."

Charlie spent the next couple of hours laying dead sticks and branches around the area where he knew that anyone sneaking up on them would have to walk; leaving a couple of areas clear for himself to come and go without being heard. After he moved the horses into the circle of sticks, he rolled into his blankets and fell asleep. Joe would warn him if anyone tried to visit the camp, unannounced, and he, also, was a light sleeper.

CHAPTER 3

Charlie was awake long before dawn. He rolled out of his blanket, noticing that Joe was watching something in the open a short ways from their camp. Charlie had a short, Apache made war bow and some very wicked tipped arrows which he gathered up as he silently moved through the trees towards the open grassland. The way Joe had looked; he knew that what he was looking at was another animal and not a human. Stringing the bow and notching an arrow, Charlie moved to the edge of the trees, keeping a larger popular between him and what he saw to be an antelope as it grazed lazily towards the stream. It was a young buck, probably newly chased from its family herd by that herd's dominant buck. Left alone, it would probably lay down somewhere just before the stream, for a nap, and go down in the morning for a drink, then continue on to the other side and east.

There was a light cloud cover which showed the antelope but kept the trees in shadows. Instinctively, Charlie sighted on the antelopes forward shoulders; then back about 6 inches to its heart. He steadied the bow and let the arrow slip from his fingers. There was no sound except the low thud of the arrow as it passed through the antelope. It jumped straight up and then stopped, dazed. It died before it knew what had happened and slumped to the grass. In an hour, Charlie had it butchered and had the heart, tongue and liver on to boil over a low fire.

By the time Charlie woke again it was to the smell of cooked meat and he knew breakfast was ready. Slicing the meat into small pieces while he cooked more vegetables, Charlie made it all into a thick stew along with the fried eggs from yesterday.

The girl was still asleep but, knowing what any human wanted first thing in the morning, he went a few yards away from camp and dug a hole about a foot and a half deep; just large enough for her to sit on and not fall into it. She was awake when he returned. Signing friend and help he motioned her to watch him and, going to the hole, motioned as if he were lowering his pants and sat on the hole. She frowned but only for a second then nodded understanding. Charlie very gently picked her up and sat her over the hole, brushing back her loincloth as he did, being careful not to expose anything as he did it.

She had felt some pain, when he moved her, but had not let out a sound.

Even though beads of sweat had popped out on her face, she let a small smile come to her lips and signed friend.

Her business done, Charlie picked her up and moved her back to the bed and they ate breakfast. Again, Charlie had put herbs and medicine into her food and again, she went to sleep right after eating. Charlie gently rolled her over and exposed the wound. It had an angry fiery red look all around its edges but the stitching was strong and holding and he could see where a lot of the flesh was starting to bind together were the two sides met. After washing and bandaging it again, he took a long breath and removed all her clothing. He washed her backside and legs, leaving her on her stomach and wrapped her in the blankets so he could soak and wash her clothes.

He took some time while moving through the trees to look for any danger while carrying the girl's clothes.

He took them to the water hole and after soaking them in a bowl of water, which he made of bark; he pounded and rubbed them, loosening the stain and dirt. Then he took them, with the horses, to the stream and, while the horses drank, he cleaned her clothes with sand that he found in the water.

He continually watched the countryside for signs of danger but saw and felt nothing. Joe, also, sensed nothing out of the ordinary. They would have to move again, in a day or two, because the trips to the stream would wear a path or trail that could be easily seen by an experienced tracker.

Charlie took his time returning to camp a different way than he had yesterday; making sure that he covered his tracks wherever he could and taking the harder places where most people would not be traveling.

Back at camp, he redressed the girl and rolled her over, Charlie spent the rest of the day cooking and jerking the meat of the antelope, gathering vegetables and preparing a pack for the third horse; who he decided to call Molly. It seemed to suit her because she was so casual and accepting of her situation.

"How had that outlaw trash come to have such good natured horses?" Charlie thought. He managed to get some fishing done the next time he watered the horses so, supper was vegetables and fried fish. He would keep most of the antelope for food on the trail. Dried it would keep indefinitely and would give them a good food source that took no preparation; meaning no open fires and no stopping time, just in case they needed to run.

The girl woke about mid-afternoon so they had an early supper. As soon as she realized that her leggings were clean, she started to blush, which made Charlie very self-conscious and, in the awkwardness of the situation, made them both laugh. It seems that they were both quiet people and they were starting to learn to be comfortable and trust each other.

Charlie, after cleaning the dishes, sat down a few feet away from her and, pointing to his chest, spoke first; "Charlie. Char-lie".

She understood immediately and, pointing to her self, said "Ray" or something that sounded like that. Charlie later found out that Ray in her language meant sun beam. Her voice was soft and low, quite pleasant to Charlie's ears.

She started to talk; speaking slow and softly. A pleasant sounding language that, even though Charlie could not understand, he let her talk awhile because he liked to hear her voice. When she paused, Charlie signed that he could not understand her speech but he liked it.

She blushed again and signed that she had been talking her native tongue; Nez Pres.

Charlie tried a little English but knew immediately that she did not know it. He tried French, Apache, Cree, Spanish and about half a dozen more languages; all without success. He was not an expert at all these languages but he had picked up a working knowledge of them as his missionary parents had taken him with them on their travels.

Then He tried an older version of Delaware that he had learned a long time ago. In the East, Delaware was a very common language spoken by most of the eastern tribes. She understood some of what he said, though she did not know it very well.

With the Delaware language and with signs they made do to communicate. Charlie found out that she was a chief's daughter and that she was a long way from home. It was not long before she became exhausted and Charlie signed that they could continue another time; that she had to rest and get better. He gave her a drink of an herb and medicine broth that he had made while they had talked and watched as she relaxed in a deep sleep.

He sat there deep in thought while the afternoon passed into evening.

Ray was a Nez Pres middle chief's daughter that had been promised to a Cheyenne war chief's son to be his wife. Her tribe was hoping to establish peace between the two Indian races because their fighting had killed off a lot of their younger men. The marriage had been arranged and she was traveling to meet her future husband when her party was attacked by a band of Sioux. She had been taken captive and, she assumed, that most of her party was killed. She did not know if anyone knew she was captured or not.

The Sioux, fearing Cheyenne retaliation, had come north very quickly. They had treated Ray very rough and had hopes of selling her to whisky traders that they knew.

While passing Fort Benton, she had been with her female guard and they had fallen behind the rest of the party. They thought that she had accepted her captivity and had not tied her hands.

As they were crossing a dry wash, she had knocked the older squaw from her horse and had turned her horse to run toward the fort. She had felt the impact on her back but had kept on. She remembers riding close to the fort and could see the solders watching from the top of the wall. The Sioux were too afraid of the solders to follow her. She had ridden and hidden for a week, not knowing that she was going in circles. Fortunately for her that she had; the Sioux could not figure out where she was going and, because she crossed her own trail a number of times, could not figure out where she was.

She could not remember where she had lost her horse or how she got to the rock where Charlie had found her. She does remember seeing the three men set up the ambush for Charlie and watched him ride into it, seemingly unaware. She had watched until Charlie had ridden away and she had fainted. The next thing she remembers was waking up on the travois and then, again, here by the fire.

"Lord, what have you got me into?" Charlie laughed. He knew that nothing happened by chance and whatever he was in, he had a job to do.

Thinking out loud, he said "I could take her with me, west." But he knew that was not an option. What would he do with her then? She belonged to her people; the Nez Pres and she belonged with her future husband. Charlie didn't know if they knew she was alive or, even, if they were alive.

Oh well, south and east it was then. One step at a time and God help them. However, she was a pretty traveling companion.

An hour before sundown, Charlie took Joe and made a wide circle around their camp area looking for any sign of trouble or human activity but it seemed that the world had forgotten them. It seemed that they were alone but that changed by morning.

Charlie had been in the wild long enough to wake up quickly. He was asleep one second and awake, with his eyes and ears open, the next. He didn't move; only his eyes and ears were alert. It was about three in the morning and he knew something was near. Joe was looking at something out in the open.

Slipping out of his blankets and putting on his deerskin moccasins, Charlie slipped away in the night quiet as a shadow. He took his hand guns and shotgun, night was no place for the bigger guns. Coming to the horses, he tied a bandana around Molly's eyes and another around Nails' eyes. That would keep them from whinnying and he spoke to Joe to keep him quiet. From the direction that Joe was looking, he knew that company was coming from the west. He strained his eyes as he looked through the trees for motion or shapes that would tell him who or what was approaching.

He could hear a thump every now and again; the kind a horse's hoof will make on dirt as it walks. Then, just west and a little south of the tree-line he caught the slightest movement through the trees. The moon was out and it was lit up like daylight out on the prairie but the trees threw a constantly moving shadow inside the tree-line making Charlie's slow careful movements unperceivable by the approaching horsemen.

As he made his way to the edge of the woods, he could hear low muffled conversation and see four horsemen moving slowly by the tree island. He could tell by the way they rode that they were tired. They were heading toward the river. Charlie slipped out to the edge of the trees and listened. They were Sioux and they were confused about searching for something.

Charlie wished he could hear more but they kept moving away. That was not a bad thing but Charlie would bet a dollar to a wooden nickel that these were some of Ray's captors. She had spoken of a dozen and a few squaws, which left him wondering where the rest were.

A lot of people will tell you that the Indian will not fight at night for fear of dying and his soul not being able to find its way home but that was wishful thinking on someone's part. The truth is that the Indian is one of the best lone fighters, day or night and, one on one, able to give a very good scrap. They learned hand to hand from the time they were knee high to a small dog and were taught weapons as soon as they could hold one. They fought constantly with each other and the white man and had learned war from their elders. Charlie was not underestimating these four and, if he could avoid it, was not going to mix with them.

He pondered the situation as he watched them ride away. The river was only about a mile away and any reasonable sound would carry that far at night. Ray still should not be moved and the travois would leave a trail that a child could follow. If these waited at the river for the rest of the band, Charlie and Ray might be in a worse mess before long.

It was too close to daylight to do anything now, so Charlie decided to leave it up to God and went back to the camp. He took the bandanas off the horses and dug the water basin bigger. It might be their only source of water for awhile. Then he lay down and catnapped until daylight.

It the half light of sunrise, he cooked more vegetables and meat; making a thick stew. Then he helped Ray with her morning duty. They ate and he cleaned up the camp before he told her what he saw last night. She looked at him something like a trusting puppy would; with her rather large brown eyes and her only comment was "Trust friend."

She had watched him ride into three guns and, after killing the three, had ridden away without a scratch. She knew he was a smart and competent warrior and a caring and careful man.

He outlined his present thoughts to her; they would stay quiet throughout today, resting and watching and, by evening, they would trust God to give them some idea what to do that night.

She listened intently; nodding her agreement and approval of his decisions.

He signed that he wished to see her wound and, as he examined it, saw that it had a little pus at the worst end. It looked red and puffy but the pus was draining and there were no red lines running up or down her back, which was a good sign. Her back muscle seemed to be knitting together again but the wound would leave her with a permanent scar. Of course, horseback riding was out of the question but they could manage with the travois and could hide through the day and travel at night, if they had to.

After his examination, he made her an herb and medicine tea which put her to sleep almost at once. Then, taking his binoculars, he went to the backside of the tree island and spent half the day studying the surrounding country side. He circled the island, looking and waiting; patiently missing nothing.

By noon he knew that the four were camped at the river and a faint dust cloud told him that more were on their way from the south-west but the most disturbing thing he saw was that about an hour ago one lone Indian had come from the East on the trail that they had made when they had come here. He had gone down into the river bottom at the same place that he and Ray had. Even though it was almost a mile downriver, he would almost certainly come up to meet with the other four. So, even if the travois trail was washed out, he would be here and then there would be five and they would know that there was three dead men back east and one or two live people somewhere west of them.

"Lord, you sure are making things interesting." Charlie whispered. Charlie's decision to take Ray home would mean he would have to go through or around the Indians. No one in their right mind ever considers going through an Indian band and he could not continue west because that's where they would be looking for them. Circling to the north was still an option that Charlie was considering.

The horses were well rested, now, and were content to stay in the trees and nibble leaves and buds. Charlie chewed on a piece of jerked antelope while he considered the situation. He had been watching a front of low dark clouds, moving in from the west, for quite some time before he realized what he was looking at. Rain was coming.

Charlie started to get a really wild idea. The Indians had been looking in the east, south and southwest; so, why not hide where they had already looked. It would mean riding right through them, almost, but it might be possible if it rained hard enough and long enough. He started to study the rain clouds with a renewed interest.

They were low and dark back as far as Charlie could see and spread from South to North almost in a straight line; the blue sky ended at the dark edge and that edge was coming rather quickly. It didn't look like the cloud front was raining but everything under the clouds was hidden by the rain making it look like a gray wall topped by the dark clouds. It hid the mountains and advanced over the prairie swallowing up the grass and tree clumps as it came.

"That rain was heavy way back." Charlie thought. He started to make his plans. There were five Indians by the river now; the other band would reach them about dusk, if they continued to travel at the same speed that they had been traveling at. It was about four in the afternoon; the way the wind was picking up, the rain would get here early in the evening.

Charlie calculated on his fingers; "Rain for an hour, then the larger group arrives, soaked. They would talk and eat; another hour. Just about the darkest time before the moon gave what light it could through the clouds. How about it, Lord? Could it work?"

He didn't hear God say anything but the rain and the idea were not a coincidence.

He went to the south side of the tree island and, with his binoculars, studied the route they would have to take. If they went close enough to the Indians, they would not think to look for their tracks and by morning they would be so blurred that they could be easily overlooked.

Charlie knew right where the Indians were because they were making no effort to hide their campfire smoke. He noticed a shallow wash cutting gradually into the ground just this side of the first tree island from the river. It went down to the river, getting deeper as it went, about five hundred yards south of the Indian camp. The one they had come out of the river in was above the Indian camp and, if they tried to use it, would muddy the water that flowed by the camp. Someone was bound to see it.

"Phew" Charlie thought "That's going to be close." He saw no other way, the travois had to have that gentle slope to get to the river where they could travel in the water and further hide their trail.

The sky was getting noticeably darker with cloud cover when Charlie went back to camp and cooked supper. Ray was awake and watched him silently. As they ate, Charlie outlined his plan and how, he hoped, it would go. Then he set about breaking camp and putting the packs in order.

Joe would pull the travois; he was gentle and strong and would not be easily frightened if anything happened. He could also be trusted to carry the necessary items like the spare guns, ammunition, blankets and food. Molly would carry the camp packs and he would ride Nails. When everything was ready to be loaded on the horses, Charlie sat down beside Ray and took out a hand gun. He held it out to her and signed the question; did she understand guns. No, she signed back but signed that she would like his war bow and arrows. These she could use.

Frowning, he dug the bow and an arrow out of the pack and offered it to her. Ray smiled and signed for him to tighten the draw string one loop at each end and then pass it to her. He did as she instructed and watched in amazement as she held the bow sideways and drew the arrow across the top and notched it. She drew the arrow back almost to her breast and then, swinging just her arm, moved the bow in a circle showing Charlie her ability to aim it in almost any direction in front of her. With the bow string shortened, the bow was half drawn before she started and was almost as powerful with the short draw as with a full draw and a longer string.

Charlie smiled and nodded his approval and Ray unstrung the arrow and laid the bow beside her, quickly dropping her eyes as she smiled her pleasure at his approval.

Charlie dug out the dead men's rain slickers and covered the horses with them just as it started to rain. Ray was under the lean-to so he put his own on. He busied himself by filling the canteens and making one last check around the tree island. He stopped dead in his tracks when he reached the south side. There was the other Indian band crossing the grassy plain and heading for the very wash he and Ray were going to use. He counted five more Indian warriors, a couple of young boys and four squaws. They were going to have a village set up there tonight. They had a number of spare horses loaded down with tepees, packs and hides.

Even though they were not traveling light, you could tell they had traveled hard and fast; their horses feet were dragging slightly and they slouched as they rode. "Good," thought Charlie, "Tired people missed a lot that was going on around them."

He watched them until the last one disappeared down the wash then went back and started to load the horses. It kept raining harder and harder, as he worked. When he was ready, it was getting darker as night came on.

He signed to Ray that it was time and he gently picked her up and laid her in the travois. He knew it hurt but she never made a sound. "Tough little sprout." He thought. He wrapped one of the slickers over her and tied it down to keep her dry. The slickers were made with a slit across the back for ventilation. The top edge overlapped the bottom to keep the rain out under normal circumstances; this slit he used to cover Ray's head so that see could look out through the opening and still keep dry. He laid his bow across her body and placed the arrows beside her, within easy reach.

He would know before midnight if his plan would work; they would either be on the other side of the stream, heading for safety, dead or, Charlie shuddered slightly, worse.

CHAPTER 4

Darkness was settling in fast as they left the tree island and, using the second island as a cover, started across the grass for the wash. Urgency was pushing him, but he forced himself to go slow. A fast moving object is easier to see than one that is moving at a slower constant pace.

They reached the wash without raising an alarm and started down into it. As they progressed, it got deeper and wider. Charlie listened but all he could hear was the wind and rain. As the sides of the wash gradually progressed away from them, they grew darker and harder to see. He had to trust in his horses to pick their way safely but the bottom was worn smooth from rain runoff and was covered with grass that helped muffle any the noise that the horses made. He loosened his hand guns; making sure that they would not stick in the holsters if he needed them quick. He also rode with the shotgun across his knees. If they were discovered in here, it would be a blood bath for sure. Charlie determined that, if he had to die, he was not going alone. These were Sioux, and, if they took him alive, they would make sure that he wished he had died quick but, however fierce they might be, they also did not want to die. Sending them a sudden, deadly barrage could change their mind enough to allow them to get away. That was his plan so far.

The wind was at their backs and the driving rain encouraged the horses to drift with it.

Down the wash they drifted, expecting to be discovered at any moment but hoping not to be. The rain and darkness held his view to a couple of yards all around them.

Glancing back, he could see Joe directly behind him and just make out Molly's head. The travois was just a dark lump behind Joe. Charlie estimated that they were nearing the wash's mouth by the distance that they had traveled. There would be a short open space before they were in the bushes growing along each side of the river.

If the Indians where in their camp and the guards were not down this way very far, they should pass the village in the rain and darkness beyond their sight and undetected.

Strange, the darkness did not seem to be as thick here; the fog, made up by the colder rain landing on the sun warmed grass and soil, seemed to be getting grayer and he could make out the sides of the wash and the grass. Alarmed, he thought that the moon was coming up and that the rain clouds were thinning.

Suddenly, they burst from the wash into the river bottom. The Indians had moved their camp, because of the drive of the wind and were almost beside the wash's mouth. Their bonfire light up the night where they were eating and talking. They were only about a hundred yards from the wash's mouth and Charlie and Ray could be seen by the firelight, if the Indians looked their way.

"Shit!" Mumbled Charlie, "Sorry Lord, I meant shoot! We might need a little help here."

His tension transferred itself to Nails and he bunched, ready to jump ahead and run. Fighting his nerves, Charlie grabbed the reins and pulled Nails back; making him walk slowly forward. He leaned over Nails' neck, trying to make himself smaller looking in the saddle. He hoped anyone looking their way would mistake them for a few horses going for water.

Joe, walking a short distance behind them, did not change his pace and Molly, walking just behind Joe, almost hid the travois.

The noise from the Indian village wavered; then increased in intensity. Charlie risked a look over Nails neck. He pulled his hat low over his face and peeked out under the brim because he knew that his face would be a sharp white, reflecting the fire light, compared to the surrounding dark. The Indians were stirred up about something but they were not all looking their way. As Charlie studied them, he decided that they were in a heated discussion about something else besides them. The men were all around the fire and the excitement was electrifying.

As Charlie watched a big man, thick through the chest with muscular arms and shaggy black hair and dressed only in breeches was talking; gesturing occasionally with a violent move of his arms first one way and then the other. The motion took in first the expanse toward the east and then the southwest; the direction Charlie knew that they had traveled from. He was a passionate speaker and everyone was paying attention to his words; even the squaws who, even though it was rare, were allowed to sit in on the meeting. He seemed to be directing his words towards a group of younger men; three of whom were standing together. One would occasionally lift a hand as if to speak but was overcome by the words and passion of the big man.

The horses, however, did not seem to be drawing their attention. The rain became heavier and, here by the river, ground fog was hanging in the air. Charlie hoped that it would help hide their movement.

Each step the horses took seemed to drag into minutes, and the urge to hurry was almost overpowering. Charlie leaned out on the far side of Nails and looked back at Ray. All he could see was Joe and a dark lump behind him on the travois. Ray was not moving and Charlie wondered if she was alright or if she knew what was happening. Who would have guessed that the Indians would move their camp or that they would still be up and outside at this time of night and in this weather. All these thoughts raced through Charlie's mind and he was distracted from what was in front of him.

Half way to the river bushes, dark shapes started to rise suddenly from the ground, popping up beside them and surrounding them were the Indian's horses. They had been herding here and, as Charlie's horses moved up and into the herd, they slowly turned, one by one, and walked along with Charlie and his horses.

Casually, they moved toward the water; the herd covering Charlie's horses tracks and hiding them within the herd. Alarmed, Charlie studied the Indian village to see if the movement was noticed. He started to see more and more faces turn their way but the conversation of the big Indian kept taking their attention back to the fireside group. His passion was still rising, it seemed, and his gestures were more forceful and his voice was rising and carrying to Charlie's ears now. He caught words in Sioux that he recognized but he could not catch enough to figure out what they were arguing about.

The boys had been left to watch the herd but, in the excitement of the Indian discussion, had their attention drawn to the village and the passion of the big man. It was one of those everlasting situations that seemed to go in slow motion. Charlie was beginning to think that they would never reach the water. He expected that at any moment they would be discovered and bullets and arrows would be flying to stop them or take their lives. His shoulders stated to ache with the tension and his skin started to crawl as his nerves stretched to their breaking point.

It was like a wave that starts small and ripples out across a pond as the horses plodded casually on towards the stream. Those in front rising from the ground and starting to move as those in motion got to them and those behind shuffling along and pausing to sniff at each other or bite off a clump of grass to chew on the way. By the time the whole herd was in motion, Charlie could just make out the dark line of the bushes along the streams edge. Glancing back, he saw the Indians still in their heated discussion with more of them now on their feet. They seemed to be taking sides, some with the big man and some with the three younger men. The squaws were siding with the big man and Charlie knew that the Indians respected their women so he would probably win.

When they reached the shelter of the bushes, Charlie breathed a sigh of relief; he hadn't realized that he was holding his breath waiting to be discovered. The Indian horses seemed to welcome the company and kept pace with Charlie and his group allowing themselves to be led into the bushes and down the stream.

"This could be bad," thought Charlie, "When they notice the horses gone, they'll come looking for them, sure." He rode with his shotgun out and ready; alert to any movement other than the horses. Behind him he heard a shout and the commotion grew. He knew they had discovered their horses gone.

Because of Ray, he dared not go any faster; he had to trust that the darkness and the storm would hide them enough to give them time to get away. The wind and rain made it hard to hear any pursuit and the fog held his vision down to just the riverbank but, through the bushes, he could see the occasional burning stick as an Indian moved close to the stream looking for horse tracks. He moved the shotgun to cover these spots of light but each time they moved away again into the gray rain and fog.

They kept moving down the river; traveling in the water to hide their trail. Each minute that passed was a little more distance from the Indians. Charlie saw fewer light torches as they moved farther away from the village.

An hour later and about three miles from the Indian village, the horses left the river of their own accord and started to climb. The horses were all around them and Charlie didn't know what horse was in the lead but he knew that God was the real leader and was taking them where He wanted them to be. That hope kept Charlie calm and he followed the herd out of the water. It was a very gentle incline and Charlie figured that it had to be a game trail that led back up to the grassy plain. Stopping on the level top, Charlie rode back to Joe and jumped down to check on Ray. He knelt down and touched her face; then he leaned close, almost touching her face with his and, speaking Delaware, asked if she was alright. Her low, weak voice told him she was alright but he heard the weakness and knew that she was not alright. The movement and the cold storm had taken her strength. He took the bow and arrows and, storing them in the packs, pulled out a dry blanket and wrapped her in it. After replacing the slicker, he told her they had to continue until they found shelter and that, he hoped, it wasn't far away. She reassured him that she would be alright and for him to continue on. Doubtfully he mounted and they pushed on through the wet grass.

The rain continued to come in a heavy downpour, making the horse herd move along close beside them and in this tight group they traveled across the prairie.

Thankfully the heavy rain and driving wind was laying the grass down in the same direction that they were going so, it would all look the same and would not make the walking any more difficult. A tracker would have to be very good to find their trail in these conditions.

Every hour or so, Charlie would get down and walk beside the travois; leading Nails by his bridle rope. This kept him reasonably warm and he could keep a check on Ray's condition while he was beside her. Her fever would flare up and cool down as they traveled and that was not good; an unstable fever could turn either way at any moment and burn her up, stopping her heart from the heat and killing her before Charlie could know it and help her.

It was four more hours before they dropped down into another tree lined wash. Charlie figured they were about thirteen or fourteen miles from the Indians and about four miles south of the three dead men. "Could even be the same wash." Charlie thought, but it would have to do. The wind dropped off as they descended to the botTim and he could see the blackness of trees around them. Turning south, he kept on, moving through the trees. No longer worrying about covering their trail, he picked the easiest and fastest way to go looking for a place to stop and rest. About a mile done the wash, he discovered a sharp incline that seemed to offer some shelter from the storm with enough wood around for a fire.

While Charlie built a fire, the horses seemed content to keep close; nibbling at leaves and grass and giving the area the sounds of a stable. Funny where and when a man's mind will go as Charlie thought about the baby Jesus and His birth setting. Jesus was born in a stable and would have had the same animal sounds around Him as they had right now. The circumstances would have been somewhat the same, too; with Joseph looking after a pregnant Mary.

After getting a good, warm fire going, he built a hasty lean-to, of tree-limbs and slickers, for Ray. Going over to the travois, he leaned close and lifted the back flap. Ray was unconscious; he felt her pulse and found that it was weak so he gently lifted her and carried her over to the lean-to. Her clothes were reasonably dry so he rolled her into a couple of blankets, for warmth, and left her to sleep.

He unsaddled the horses and left them to wander. Not only were his horses staying near but the Indian horses were mixing with his and making themselves at home; strange but, who was he to question how an animal will think. As he worked, he would pat or rub what ever horse he walked by and they seemed to appreciate the attention.

Next, he unpacked just what they needed. He tried to leave as much as he could packed and ready for a hasty escape; just in case they needed to get away quick.

The rain had slowed to a steady drizzle and the wind was dying down. By daylight, he knew, the Indians would be looking for their horses and they could travel almost as fast, on foot, as a horse could at a fast walk. Charlie's advantage lay in the fact that the Indians did not know where he was or what direction they had taken but, with that many Indians, they would probably fan out in all the logical directions which could mean at least two or three would travel this way. He knew that horses will drift with the wind in a storm and so would the Indians. They would find their trail; it was just a matter of time but, for now, they were safe. The Indians could not follow them in the dark and under these conditions and by morning, when they started to look for their horses, he and Ray would be moving away from them again.

It was about three in the morning and Charlie curled up in a dry blanket, after putting more wood on the fire, and fell asleep.

He was awake again at five and, after rebuilding the fire, checked on Ray. She seemed to be sleeping and her pulse was stronger. He put together a hasty breakfast and woke her. After their morning requirements and breakfast, he let her go back to sleep while he checked on the horses. Twenty-five all together; one for each Indian, their six pack animals and Charlie's three. If it hadn't been for the storm, they would have left a trail that a blind man could have followed. The way it was, a very good tracker might be able to follow them but he would have to be good; very good.

Charlie wasn't going to wait to find out if they were being followed. He saddled the horses and repacked the packs, loading them on the horses. He had been followed by a young, three year-old mare while he had prepared the horses so he built a small pack and tried it on her; just to see and, maybe, lighten Molly's load a little. She took it like she enjoyed it so he left it on her.

He placed Ray back on the travois and she didn't wake up. That told him that she was pretty worn down so they would have to get to a safe place soon.

They were ready by seven o'clock, which was a little later than he wanted to leave but it could not be helped; the sun had been up for two hours and, he guessed, so were the Indians.

It had the promise of clearing and becoming a sunny day, however, for now, the ground was still wet and they left lots of tracks wherever they went. Charlie worried over that and pushed a little harder, trying to put some distance away from that spot, quickly, knowing that it was just a matter of time before the Indians found it. He was ahead on Nails and Joe followed with the travois with the rest bunched up behind them. This would hide the travois' track somewhat, at least. When the Indians found their trail, they might think that there were more people and go slower with caution; giving Ray and him a little more time.

The land was still rolling plains and Charlie tried to keep in the lower places and stay off the sky line. It slowed them down, switching back and forth, following the lower places but they raised no dust with the ground still damp and, he hoped, that, if the Indians could not see them that they would waste some time searching in other directions.

As they traveled, Charlie kept a sharp eye, not only on their back trail but all around them. The Sioux behind them were not the only Indians that traveled these parts. The Black Foot raided here and the Cheyenne could be found here occasionally. If any Indians saw them first, they could lay in wait somewhere ahead of them and could suddenly appear from the ground right beside them and could make for a hasty defense. Such a surprise was not what Charlie wanted right now.

By mid-afternoon, he knew that the Indians had found their trail. He had seen movement on his back-trail for the last hour now and the stealth that they used was defiantly Indian. Being on foot, they would not catch them easily but it meant that they could not stop for long to rest and the Indians had sent up a smoke talk which would bring the others this way. Also, if there were anymore in the area that saw the smoke, they would be coming this way, too. Charlie now had to worry that they might blunder into an ambush or be taken over from either side by Indians on horses. There was no advantage, now, to follow the low places and he rode a straight line away from those following. It was no longer a hide and seek; but a race to safety. Where the ground was reasonably smooth, he tried putting the group into a trot; watching the travois to make sure that Ray was not bounced around too much. Joe had a very smooth canter and kept the travois steady. He was one of the smartest horses Charlie had ever seen and he seemed to know that he had to be careful for the human in the blankets behind him and traveled where the ground was the smoothest or were the grass would cushion the ride.

Charlie had been traveling south east, hoping to get to the Missouri river at a little place called Coal Banks Landing. His hopes were to rent a boat or find a steam ship and go down the river into Nebraska, where they could head back west again into Colorado. Here was where Charlie planned to start his search for Ray's people but, first, they had to get there.

The next wash they went down into ran almost straight north and south. It had a dry grassy bottom and looked almost like a readymade road. It was also deep enough to hide them from the eyes of the Indians following them. Charlie turned south, in the wash, but traveled slowly enough so that they would not stir up a dust cloud; the grass had dried with the sun and he did not want the Indians to know that he had turned. He knew that Fort Benton was almost due south and hoped to find safety there because it was closer. Tired as they were, the Indians were still able men and not to be taken lightly. They were tough and could stay on a fast track until they dropped from exhaustion.

He had wrapped Ray's back up for traveling and he had left a pad over the pus opening but, after another couple of hours traveling, he stopped and checked her wound. It was draining pus and blood and her pulse was weak. It would take another eight or nine hours to reach the fort; long past midnight, if they kept up this pace. Charlie had to decide whether to try and outrun the Indians by not stopping or, if Ray could not go on, to stop and ambush them.

"Not much of a choice, Lord." Charlie commented "Possibly lose Ray or kill some people. Hum. No real choice at all." He decided to continue on at the same pace and hope for an answer later.

Traveling in the wash meant that Charlie could not see what was happening up on the plains. He could not guess that they would soon have company in the wash that would change everything. He kept moving south, fearing to stop because of the pursuit and worrying because he could not see anything. He did not know how close they were or if any more were around. The horse herd made it hard to hear any other sounds. Charlie was just on the verge of stopping and checking the plain or, he thought, possibly going insane because his senses had been warning him that something was wrong for a little while now.

Coming around a gentle bend, he saw that the wash took a sudden sharp turn just ahead and brush had collected on the left side from runoff water bringing it down and depositing it in the eddy of the turn. The bank was indented on the right side making a cave big enough for a camp site. The water had hit it quite hard because the banks were closer and higher here.

Charlie was considering a brief stop when he heard "Halt! Stop right there!" The voice had the snap of command behind it. Looking up Charlie saw the head and shoulders of a soldier who was standing on the top of the bank; rifle pointed casually at them almost to his shoulder. He could sight and fire from that position in a split second, if he had to.

"Captain of the guard!" shouted another soldier on the other bank. "Strangers in the wash!"

Charlie relaxed and, in a few minutes, three soldiers came around the brush pile, rifles ready, and came up to Charlie. A rather young lieutenant in the lead asked "Who are you and where are you going?"

Charlie replied, "My name is Charlie and I'm right glad to see you boys."

Carefully, so they would know his intent, Charlie put his shotgun into its scabbard. They waited and Charlie continued, "I have a hurt girl on the travois and a dozen Sioux trailing us. If you don't mind, we would like to join you for supper."

The lieutenant smiled at the supper comment but said, "I would be after you, too, if you stole my horses" as he obviously looked past Charlie to the horse herd.

"Sorry, lieutenant, but they just kind of followed me here. They like my company, I guess; you don't see any lead rope on them, do you?"

"You have a point, young man." And it was Charlie's turn to smile; he figured that he and the lieutenant were about the same age. The friendly banter relaxed the men and they lowered their guns. The lieutenant continued, "You said that you have an injured girl?"

"Yes, she's on the travois. It's been almost a day since she's had any medicine or rest from traveling. She has a nasty knife wound across her back and, with running from the Indians; it has started to bleed again. If you could give us a safe place to rest, we would appreciate it."

"Of course." Was the reply, "Come this way." And he turned and went back around the brush pile. Charlie felt his body relaxing with the added security of the Army so near.

CHAPTER 5

Once on the other side, Charlie saw that the wash opened into a small valley and the soldiers had a camp set up for the night. The valley was about five hundred yards long and about two hundred yards wide at its widest point. Halfway down the middle there was a growth of poplars surrounding a pool of water left over from the rains that kept it fed year round. From there the sloop started gradually upward to the flat prairie floor above; getting noticeably steeper as it got closer to the top.

There were sixteen soldiers in sight which made about twenty or more altogether by Charlie's guess; too many for the dozen Sioux unless they got a lot of reinforcements. They had two fires going where the cook wagon was parked and Charlie could smell hot coffee that was on constantly while they were stopped, so the guards changing in the night could have a cup when they wanted one. The men were scattered in a circle around the camp in various stages of preparation for the night's stay here but were all still up and watching

Charlie's band of horses as they approached. Their own horses were herded between the camp and the poplars. Charlie caught the flash of light off a gun barrel on the top of the sloop to his right and suspected that there were more guards on both sides of the sloop further down the valley.

As the lieutenant walked into camp he called, "Sergeant, there are Sioux about; inform the guards to stay alert." Immediately a rough looking sergeant stood up and turned to a couple of men and started speaking to them. Turning to Charlie, the lieutenant continued. "Charlie, you and your girl can set up here, in the middle of camp. Our doctor is back at the fort but we have a few medical supplies with us. Baker," he turned his head and looked at a neatly dressed soldier beside one of the fires. "Bring up what medical supplies we have and give Charlie whatever he needs." Baker saluted sharply and climbed into the wagon. You could hear him moving around inside while he found the supplies.

Charlie immediately started to make a place for Ray. With the help of the soldiers, Charlie had her on a soft pile of horse blankets and bedding in no time. They were eager to help, especially when they saw how pretty Ray was. The sergeant, after sending word of the Indians to the sentries, hovered over Ray and him like a mother hen; trying to help in any way he could. He laughingly told the story about his nickname, which was Toddy; he was in love with this girl but was shy so, when it was time to go see her, he would go down to the bar and have a few toddies of whisky for courage.

"It must have worked," he said "'Cause, I've been happily married now for the last dozen years and got two of the prettiest kids you ever saw. I don't drink anymore but the boys won't let me off with any other nickname. My real name is Todd McKinley but you folks just go ahead and call me "Toddy"."

This brought a round of laughter from the soldiers and, even though she did not understand, Ray smiled and enjoyed the revelry. It was a weak smile showing her condition after the travois ride.

The lieutenant, coming up just then, opened his mouth to say something but stopped short, his mouth open, and stared at Ray. Closing his mouth and looking hastily at Charlie he said, "She's an Indian." The men stopped laughing and the tension was almost physical in the silence.

Quickly, Charlie replied, "A Nez Pres, to be exact. They've been our friends for a long time now. They're at war with the Sioux and she had been their captive until a little while ago." He had just learned something about the lieutenant that he wished he hadn't learned. He was an Indian hater and not really well liked by his men.

The lieutenant thought on that a minute and, with a shrug, continued, "We're heading out from the fort; got away a little late so we didn't get far. We are to scout to the northwest and make a swing back north and northeast looking for some renegade Sioux that central command said left raiding in Colorado about a month ago and headed this way."

Charlie commented, "I guess they are going to find you. They're probably the same ones that are chasing us. Ray," Charlie waved his hand in Ray's direction, "told me she was captured around Colorado and came northwest with this bunch. They killed her party and were going to sell her to whiskey traders."

Charlie didn't like this kind of business of the white man trying to control the Indians; trying them and punishing them for things that they had done all their lives and thought were normal. Live with them, eat with them and, if need be, fight with them, fine; but don't send them to live on reservations or send them to a white man's jail. If they kill whites, shoot them but, if they don't, leave them alone. He didn't voice his opinion out loud and didn't let it show on his face.

The explanation seemed to satisfy the lieutenant and eased the tension in the camp. Charlie noticed the sergeant giving him a serious and thoughtful look; taking in Charlie's easy confident mannerisms and the way he wore his weapons.

Charlie turned and went back to tending to Ray; making sure that she was comfortable and helping her to get a drink of water. She smiled her thanks and Charlie heard the lieutenant's sharp intake of breath behind him. He knew that Ray's good looks had made an impression on him. The cook brought a bowl of stew that smelled good so Charlie sat down and helped her eat. She cleaned out the bowl and the cook refilled it. She emptied that bowl three more times.

While Charlie had been tending to Ray, the soldiers had unsaddled their horses and put them in their Ramada to be watched with their own horses by the night guard. Charlie noticed the sergeant moving through his men and talking to one or another making sure that nothing came of the situation that had reared its ugly head in the exchange.

Charlie took Ray for her necessary business and stayed with her until she had no more immediate needs, then he made a special point of finding the soldiers that had tended to their horses and thanked them. He showed them that he appreciated the things that they did for him. He also stopped and spent a few minutes talking with Toddy. He liked the man and found him open and friendly. His looks and mannerisms told Charlie that he was a veteran and was used to handling trouble. His speech had given him away as being Irish and what Charlie knew of the Irish was that they were an honest and tough bunch; good friends and really bad enemies.

When he could get away, he came back and sat beside Ray and ate some of the stew that the cook kept bringing.

She watched him with approval. She knew she was with a real man. One, who appreciated help, looked after his friends and his animals first and looked after his own needs later.

Charlie frowned; he read the signs correctly. Ray was getting attached to him and that was not good. Another thing that bothered him was that the lieutenant sat a short ways away and could not seem to be able to keep his eyes off Ray. Her dark hair and braids framed her face and, in the firelight, it had a radiating angelic look when she smiled at Charlie. As much as he needed sleep, Charlie thought it best if he found out a little more about this lieutenant so he moved over and sat beside him.

"I'd like to thank you for giving us some company right now." He started "Getting to Fort Benton could have done Ray in."

"You haven't told us about her wound." The lieutenant said accusingly.

"No, I haven't. She was knifed while she was escaping from the Sioux. Cut her back pretty bad. I had to do some field surgery on her and hide her so she could mend. They came close to finding us day before yesterday and we were running from them when we got here. I'm hoping to lay over in Fort Benton until she heals."

"She belong to you?" he asked. He was suggesting that Charlie had bought or traded for her and that she might be Charlie's possession or squaw.

"Nope." Charlie drawled "I'm sorry; I didn't catch your name."

"Arthur. Arthur Belmont. These westerners have been trying to stick me with Art." The lieutenant said. "I'm from Massachusetts and my mother was very fussy about me being called "Arthur"."

Aside from the fact that he was taken with Ray, Arthur seemed like a nice guy. Charlie hoped his interest in Ray was just a surface thing and would end soon but he did not have the respect of his men which told him that there was more to this than he knew. "If you don't mind, Arthur suits me. I'm not army and "lieutenant" sounds pretty formal."

"Sure" he said, "It's better than trying Art" and they both laughed. Ray had been watching them and she smiled when they laughed. Arthur's laughter took on a funny, strained note and ended.

Charlie had learned enough to know that he would have to watch Arthur. He was an Indian hater and he had a fixation for Ray; this meant that he wanted her in his bed but thought her little more than an animal, something to throw away when he was done with her. Arthur would probably not agree with Charlie's diagnoses but, whether he would admit it to himself or not, that's what Arthur would do.

Charlie stood up and stretched. "If you don't mind, Arthur, I will need a few minutes of privacy to clean and bandage Ray's wounds again."

A little too quickly Arthur blurted, "Do you need some help, I should learn a little about battle wounds."

It was all Charlie could do to keep from back-handing him. With a surgeon to learn from at the fort; him! Offering to learn from a stranger just to see some of Ray's naked flesh, was so lame that Charlie started away before he had time for his sudden flash of anger to show on his face. Over his shoulder he growled, "I can get it, *thanks.*"

If Arthur heard the sarcasm in Charlie's voice, he did not let on and Charlie figured it was wasted.

Ray saw him coming and noticeably brightened. He signed that he wanted to check her wound and it would help if she just relaxed. He did not want it to start bleeding again. She did as she was told and Charlie found that she was easy to work with. She yielded to his touch as he rolled her over. Carefully he raised her shirt, just enough to expose her wound. Studying it, Charlie was pleased to see that the redness was fading to a pink and that a scab had formed over the whole wound.

"Very good," thought Charlie. He took some of the aloe vera juice that was in the medical supplies that Baker had given him and pasted a good bit of it over the wound; then, after putting some clean pads on it, wrapped it tight again. Then he gently rolled Ray back over. She stared up at him with that same trusting and open look and Charlie felt the uncomfortable weight of his responsibility towards her getting heavier.

Just then, Charlie caught the movement of a shadow out of the corner of his eye. Grabbing the old bandages he quickly turned and threw them into the fire, looking up as he did it, he was fast enough to catch Arthur reseating himself. He had been standing, looking over Charlie's shoulder from beside the fire. Charlie pondered the speed with which Arthur's obsession was taking over.

Yawning and stretching, he said, "Well, it's been a long day; do you mind if I put this fire out so Ray and I can get some sleep. We will go to the fort in the morning but, just in case the Indians are still around, I better be alert."

"No, not at all," replied Arthur, standing up but making no move to go away.

Taking the old coffee in the pot, Charlie pored it on the fire; almost getting Arthur's boot.

Arthur seemed to come out of his fixation then and moved toward one of the other fires, calling "Good night, see you in the morning," as he went.

"In the morning," Charlie replied but he wondered. Rolling into his blanket, he laid his handguns, one on each side under the blanket. He was soon asleep.

Charlie woke with a feeling that something was not right. He lay still, not moving while he listened. Everything seemed alright but, when he moved his head slightly to look towards Ray, he caught movement out of the corner of his eye. A shadowy figure was coming across the camp site, heading towards their sleeping area.

The camp was asleep and the fires were out. The moon was casting shadows as the clouds passed in front of it so Charlie was not sure of what he saw yet. He estimated the time to be about one in the morning. The camp should be still but there was that movement again. Something or someone was coming by him; being careful to try and not wake him. It looked like a man and he was heading for Ray.

Charlie's guns were well oiled tools and when he pulled the hammer back on his handgun, it made no sound. That audible, click-click sound you normally hear means that the owner of that gun did not look after it very well. The sound was made by the metal tab, connected to the trigger mechanism sliding into place behind the lock on the hammer; it only made the click-click sound if it was dry but, if it was well oiled, there was no sound.

Charlie had the premonition that there was more going on tonight but he could not see anything but this man which crept closer and closer to Ray. She did not move and Charlie could tell she was fast asleep by her steady, rhythmic breathing. Charlie watched the man approach her and wondered how to handle the situation. This was no Indian; an Indian hunts game and men so, when he walks, he just sort of glides. You don't hear any sound except, maybe, the rustle of clothing or the scrape of buckskin on grass or skin. This man was clumping with his feet, snapping twigs and disturbing stones; maybe alright for a city slicker but Charlie thought it was terribly noisy walking.

"What do I do, Lord?" Charlie prayed. The man was beside Ray, now, and was reaching his hand for her head; possibly to cover her mouth, when Charlie decided he had better say something.

He didn't get the chance; a voice he recognized as Todd's and coming from somewhere above his head so he could not see him said, "Nice evening for a stroll, Sir."

Arthur came to an abrupt halt, pulling his hand back and stammered, "Ah, yes. It is. Ah, I was just checking on the girl to make sure she was alright."

"I'm sure you found her well, Sir." Todd remarked.

"Yes. Yes, she seems to be OK, but you can not be too careful; this is Indian country and she is one of *them*. No doubt they will want their little friend back with them." Was Arthur's lame reply, "You should be sleeping, we will probably have to run them down tomorrow."

"Yes, Sir, and we will catch them; if not tomorrow, soon. They have no horses and cannot hide forever. They may even be close by, trying to get their horses."

"Don't be absurd. We have twenty soldiers here; they wouldn't stand a chance." Arthur answered Todd. He was starting to relax and get his courage back so he blustered a little.

Todd's reply was getting a bit edgy, "Sir, these are Sioux and no one can predict what they will think or do. They are good fighting men and have won battles in the past by doing the unexpected. Also, they are not the only danger around here right now." He paused and Arthur waited; starting to sense that there was a word of wise advice coming. Todd continued, "You are in the dangerous position, right now, of being a dead man real fast."

Arthur noticeably started and with an angry voice growled, "What are you getting at, Sergeant? Are you threatening me? You have that rifle pointed in the wrong direction, if you are. I can pull my handgun and shoot you while you are turning and cocking it."

"No, Sir." Todd casually replied, "If you had noticed anything about Charlie, here, you would know that he has been living in

Indian country for some time and he is not someone you can sneak up on. The way he wears his guns also tells you that he is a very dangerous man to anger. I would guess that, probably within the next second or two, you would have gotten a bullet somewhere in or near your heart. Am I right Charlie?"

Charlie's answer was low and almost a growl, "He was asking for that, for sure."

Arthur noticeably started again and took a step back. He had been caught and he knew it.

Just then, the moon came out from behind the clouds and you could see that Arthur's face was as white as a sheet. Charlie knew then that he was not going to admit anything and that, if they stayed close to each other past tomorrow morning, that he would have to cripple or kill Arthur. He gave him an easy out tonight by saying, "It's late, gentlemen, and we all have work to do tomorrow. It would be wise to get some more sleep before sunrise."

Todd supported with, "That's good advice, Charlie; after you, Sir." His voice was like iron and left no room for a negative answer.

Arthur turned away, stumbling slightly as he walked back to his bedroll. Toddy spoke low so that only Charlie heard him, "Try to get away tomorrow without killing him, please. He is still my commanding officer and I still have to look out for him."

"I'll try; as long as he doesn't try to interfere with us leaving he should be OK. I would hate to have to tangle with you, Toddy. I think I would have my hands full with that chore." Charlie spoke with genuine warmth; liking this big Irishman.

"Thank you. I know you would have your hands full with me and I would have my hands full with you. Wouldn't that be something to see?" Then he answered himself with, "but the days of me enjoying myself with a little scrap or two now and again are gone. Me little wife would hang me out to dry in a blink if she knew I was scraping again. Good night, Charlie."

"'night, Toddy," came his reply.

CHAPTER 6

After they had left, Charlie rolled out of his blankets and, after a quick check of Ray and finding her still asleep, faded into the night for a little look around. He had put on his moccasins and was as silent as a shadow and as invisible as the thin air.

The moon had gone behind the clouds again and it hinted of more rain. He watched as Arthur and Todd each rolled up in their bed rolls and fell asleep.

Charlie made a complete circle inside the perimeter of the camp, making sure to be extra careful going by Todd but he found everyone sleeping. Next, he widened his circle and, when he came to the horses, moved easily in among them. He hummed in a low droning tone that would be missed by most as insect noise but that the horses would hear and not be frightened by his movements.

He cared very much for animals so, as he passed through the herd, he would touch a rump here and pat a nose there; always with a gentle but firm hand. By the time he came to Joe, Nails and the Indian mare were following him.

He spent a couple of minutes patting and rubbing Joe. Scratching his neck and talking to him in his low soothing voice. Joe leaned a little into his hand and rubbed his arm and shoulder with his nose. All the time Charlie spent with the horses, he was constantly looking around the area and it paid off. He had located two of the night guards by the time he moved away from them. Under Todd's command, they were alert and ready so Charlie had to be a little more careful as he slipped out of the soldiers' campsite area and onto the grassy plain.

Moving stealthily through the grass, being careful not to step on a snake or disturb the night birds, Charlie started a wide circle of the wash area; eyes and ears busily sorting out the sights and sounds and identifying each one. Each step he took could bring him death by the soldiers, not knowing he was outside the camp, or from the Indians, who Charlie was sure were in the area. They had no horses and they knew that escape from the soldiers would be difficult without them. They knew that they would have to make some attempt to get their horses or be caught by the soldiers. How many there would be was anybody's guess.

The clouds occasionally drifting in front of the moon helped him; as the shadows moved over the prairie he moved with them and became a part of them. The grass moved with the breeze and as long as he didn't move constantly in a straight line but erratically like the shadows and wind, he remained undetected.

He had slipped past the third guard and was close to where he estimated the fourth to be when he saw a bush with more shadow than it should have and it didn't move with the breeze like the real bush's shadow did.

"That was an Indian trick, not a white man's," Charlie thought and he squatted down to skyline whatever was there. It was still below his sight but the outline was that of a man, so he waited. He had been traveling in a circle with the camp on his left and, after a few minutes, he heard a low cough from the guard. He was on the edge of the wash, standing on something that Charlie could not see but with his head, shoulders and chest above the edge, screened by tall grass and bushes.

55

The shadow was getting smaller as the Indian bunched himself to start sneaking ahead again. Two more shadows, moving off to the side of the first and about thirty feet apart were coming through the grass. With the clouds, the way Charlie could see them was because they were darker than the grass that they were traveling through. The one closest to Charlie was going to pass within ten feet of him.

Charlie watched their advance and knew that they were going to make a move to get the horses. If Charlie had not been here, that fourth guard would have died. The Indians were concentrating on the guard and did not see Charlie slowly easing his way forward to get within striking range of the first Indian.

Closer and closer they moved toward each other; the Indian looking slightly away from Charlie at the guard and Charlie, easing through the grass and not making a sound, moved towards the Indian. There was a bush just in front of Charlie that was about four feet high and as Charlie reached one side of it; the Indian was just going by the other with his back to Charlie, fully concentrating on the guard.

Charlie had learned about hand-to-hand fighting from a young oriental man from some island in the Pacific Ocean, close to China.

Lin Wa, the oriental, had worked in an eating house as a chore boy in the gold camp that Charlie had stayed in. Charlie had befriended him and found him to be a very knowledgeable fellow. They had become good friends and when Charlie had almost been beaten in a fist-fight, by the town bully, Lin had taken Charlie aside and he taught Charlie the fighting habits passed down to him from his ancestors. He also taught Charlie about the bodies pressure points that, when struck, would render a person immobile or unconscious. In return, Charlie had taught Lin how to handle guns and was surprised at how fast he learned how to handle a six-gun.

Charlie now hoped that it worked on Indians as well as white men because if he alerted the other two that he was there, he was in a lot of trouble. He would also alert the guard, if he made any sound.

He took a deep breath, slide noiselessly around the bush and, before the Indian knew anyone was there, hit him on the back of his neck with the back edge of his hand, tensing his work hardened hand muscles so that they were as hard as a hammer and just a little off center so he would not break his spine.

"Ow," thought Charlie, "tough as an old piece of leather." But he had the satisfaction of seeing him, silently, slump to the ground; the impact noise being lost in the sudden gust of wind that blew by them just then. Taking his place and advancing with the other Indians, Charlie started moving slightly sideways as well as ahead, closing the gap between him and the second Indian.

Suddenly, the far Indian looked back and twittered like a night bird. The second twittered also and looked at Charlie. Charlie didn't hesitate; he too twittered. They seemed to accept that and turned back to the guard, who had stood up to investigate the sound.

The Indians waited, not wanting to move and alert him to their presence while Charlie, moving like the grass was blown by the night breezes, slipped up beside the second Indian. He was just turning his head to look at Charlie when Charlie hit him catching him just behind his temple with the big middle knuckle of his doubled-up fist.

He also slumped without a sound but the movement had caught the attention of the guard. He was staring at them trying to understand what he was looking at. They seemed to be shadows that kept changing when the clouds moved in front of the moon.

The first Indian was totally occupied with the guard and did not know what had happened behind him. The guard saw the motion and raised his rifle; still trying to understand because he heard no sound and nothing else was happening. At two thirty in the morning on a breezy, cloudy night, he was not sure if, maybe, his eyes were playing tricks on him.

Everyone seemed to be holding their breath, waiting. The soldier lowered his rifle slightly; then a little more. After ten full minutes, he again lowered his rifle more and started to look around a bit; convinced that he had been seeing things.

Charlie knew he had to act now; the first Indian would turn any second and see what was going on. Crouching below the level of the grass, he took three steps and swung; catching the Indian on the jaw just as he was turning his head.

The Indian had been crouching in the grass and Charlie's rush had been low so the soldier, looking off to the side, only saw motion and, as he turned back, Charlie squawked like a bird and moved a bush three feet to his right with his toe. By this time, the soldier, even though he thought, now, it was a bird, decided to come out and investigate.

"Lord, you do make things interesting," Charlie thought; as he slid into a slight depression a little ahead and to the left of the down Indian. The soldier had his attention on the bush that Charlie had moved and was slowly moving toward it. If he stayed to his present course, he would pass about five feet to Charlie's right.

The soldier crept forward warily, passing Charlie's position and coming to the bush, he stooped down to look into it. In a split second Charlie was beside him and, using his gun and coming under the brim of his hat, knocked him cold with a tap to his forehead. "He'll have a black eye and a nice lump for that one," thought Charlie.

Working quickly, Charlie tangled his feet in a bush and laid his rifle and arms as if he had tripped and fallen. Then he found a rock and put it under his head at the same place that Charlie had hit him. "Hope this works," Charlie mused.

Charlie worked quickly, tying the Indian's hands behind their backs and carrying them over the wash lip and out of sight. Then he slapped the first Indian he had hit, hard, waking him. Shaking him, he spoke, "Don't struggle. Listen to me." Low enough not to be heard far away but loud enough for the Indian to hear, he continued in Sioux, "I have no quarrel with my Sioux friends and will help you get your horses but you must leave and not bother the girl or these soldiers. Do you understand? Who is your leader here and who is your chief?"

The man straightened a little and spoke. "I am the leader. I am Great Bear. I understand; but who could shame us so and expect us not to fight?"

"If you do as I say and not make me send you to The Great Spirit's hell, you can tell your children that you were one with Talking Fire Hand, son of Talking Hand, tonight."

Great Bear gasped, "I have heard around the council fires of our elders that Talking Hand is the friend of the Sioux and his tongue tells the story of The Great Spirit from the book in his hand. He lives his life the same as the words say to live and his hands are gentle to my people, making sickness leave, and his heart is tender to us, living with us, hunting with us and hurting for our fallen. These stories are also with others besides the Sioux. It is also said that, not only is his son, Talking Fire Hand, like him but, when he is angry, fire comes from his hands and kills all his enemies."

Charlie answered him, "These stories are true. Who else could knock down a Sioux warrior and a Yellow leg at the same time and not kill either one needlessly. If The Great Spirit were not with me, could I do such things?" Yellow Leg was the Indian name for the United States Army soldiers, because of the single yellow strip down each leg of their uniform, and Charlie said this, not to brag, but to get Great Bear's confidence quickly; time was running out.

"Truly, you speak well," Admitted Great Bear, "The soldiers would surely catch us if we don't have our horses and they are many while we are few. If The Great Spirit has sent you to help us get our horses back, we will do as you say."

"I can see why you are the leader, Great Bear; anger is not your friend and wisdom is in your words." Charlie said, as he untied him. He noticed that it was the same big Indian that had spoken with so much passion in the Indian's camp as he and Ray rode by it. The others were awakened and, when they were all able, moved down to the bottom of the wash so that they would not be detected.

As the three hankered together, Charlie told them where the horses were and how, he thought, that they could get them without waking the camp. Charlie would walk in among the horses and, with some short pieces of rope that he would cut from one of his lariats, lead them out four and five at a time. That way, if he was caught, he was a white man and they were considered to be his horses. It sounded fine to the Indians, who were still a little awed by the fact that they were being helped by Talking Fire Hand.

They split up and, as the Indians went into the edge of the poplars below the horses, Charlie went to his packs and dug out two of the dead men's ropes. As he walked back towards the horses, he cut the rope into hackamore size pieces. He would let the Indians fashion the hackamores; he just tied a slip knot at the end of each one and made them into loops to go around the horses necks so they could be led.

He was careful not to make a noise or be seen but, as part of the camp, he was not worried so much about that. He was still hoping to be finished before the unconscious soldier came too and staggered into camp; if he staggered into camp. He might raise a noise to draw attention and then his plan would become more difficult.

He slowly moved into the herd of horses and picked some of the older, quieter Indian horses. He came out with five that seemed to walk along quietly and he took them down the wash to the waiting Indians, careful to walk to the opposite side to the other guard that was somewhere on the other lip of the wash. They came out of the brush like shadows and took the horses; fashioning hackamores for them, one Indian led them down the wash farther from the camp while the other two waited for Charlie to bring more. Charlie soon returned with six more and again they were taken down the wash by the second Indian to be held by the first. Only Great Bear remained to wait for Charlie. He was just returning with six more when they heard the brush moving where the soldier had been on guard. He was awake and staggering around. These six were quickly taken away and Charlie told Great Bear that he had better go to the soldier so he could divert the soldiers' attention away from the horses. He would make enough noise to cover Great Bear so he could get the rest of their horses and leave.

Before he went, Charlie told Great Bear that the soldiers were sent to look for them and that they were supposed to take them back to Colorado. He suggested that maybe the Sioux should make their own decision to return to Colorado and not let the white man force them back and, if they decide to go back, they could probably go south and then east again, through the river water, around Fort Benton. He suggested that the white men might not think that they would do that.

Great Bear shook his head and said, "Truly the Great Spirit is in you. You have thought of a way that we can be safe and not anger the whites more. My friend you are welcome in my tepee at any time."

Charlie said, "And you in mine, my brother; may the Great Spirit go with you and make your path easy and safe." And, then, slipped away to the lip of the wash where Todd was just getting to the soldier.

He was sitting down on the lip with his head in his hands.

Charlie heard Todd say, "Whoa, Bill, what's with you now?" and "Where is your rifle?"

Bill answered, "ow, my head! Sarg., don't shout! I busted my head on a rock and it hurts like h..heck." He had seen Charlie ask God's blessing on his food and now, when he saw Charlie come up behind Todd, he corrected himself because of Charlie.

Todd snuffed and said, "What was you doing dragging your big old head on the ground for anyway?"

Charlie had been careful to position himself so that he could see the horses and put the others so their backs were to them. He saw Great Bear leaving with the last of their horses. He was also careful not to look directly at the horses so the others would not know he was not looking at them. From their vantage point high on the lip of the wash, he could also see that they had the full attention of the other three guards. The camp could not see the Indians past the horse herd and anyone awake was looking towards the commotion at the top.

Bill moaned, "Ow. Give me a minute, Sarg. I was on guard and I heard some birds calling; then I saw one of them and it sounded like a snake got it or something. Anyway, I went over there to see and, I guess, I got my feet caught in some brush and fell on a rock. My head hurts and, I guess, this is blood on my hands. There's also a lump the size of my fist on my face."

By this time, the Indians were gone and Charlie breathed a sigh of relief. "They got away this time." He thought but he said, "Let me take a look, Bill. Yes, you've got a nice knot on your forehead. If you want to take him back to camp and patch him up a bit, Sergeant, I'll finish the rest of his watch."

"No you don't. I'll finish his watch. You can take him back to camp. Get Baker to put something on his head and then he can get some sleep." Todd said as he started over the lip to find Bill's rifle. His last words were barely audible to Charlie and missed by Bill entirely, "You ain't got much sleep yourself tonight."

As surprised as Charlie was, he grinned. He liked that Irishman and he now knew that Todd was also up and watching last night. How much he knew, Charlie could only guess but as long as the Indians were away and Todd was not saying anything, he was happy to leave it at that.

Bill was a slender youth, light of weight as well as complexion and he put his arm around Charlie's shoulders for support while he helped Bill back to camp where he found a few others were up also. They were changing the guards and one of the ones that were up was Baker. Charlie left Bill with Baker and went to his own blankets. Arthur didn't even look at him when they had come in. He started questioning Bill right away.

Ray was still asleep, which was a good sign. She was getting some much needed rest; she would need it for tomorrow. Charlie rolled into his blankets and was soon asleep.

By morning the mood in camp had changed. Charlie woke before anyone else and put his boots on; slipping his moccasins into his saddlebag again. There was the hint of grey in the east and, when he had his fire going; Todd came strolling into camp from guard duty. He grinned and winked at Charlie as he walked by but he didn't speak. He continued on to the soldiers' cook fire where the men were moving about their morning chores; hastily packing personal belongings and bedrolls in preparation to break camp. He was sober and sounded professionally serious when he reported to Arthur that the Indians had snuck into the horse herd and made off with their own horses last night.

The camp mood change obviously came from Arthur. He was surly and snapped at Todd when he heard the news about the horses. "How could they do that? The guards were not paying attention, were they? We'll just see about this." He kept mumbling as he went off to do his morning business. The rest of the men kept their heads down, watching the things that they were doing and only a few looked up to watch the Lieutenant leave.

The word was spreading quickly through the men about the incident last night between Arthur, Todd and Charlie and there were more than a few sideways looks at Charlie and Ray.

Charlie started to go through his packs for some breakfast when the cook came over and said, "Just you never mind, young feller. I cook a good meal and especially breakfast, so, you and the girl just get ready and set up with us. I'm Simon Peters but they call me Flapjack, if you want to know and don't you pay any mind to the lieutenant. He gets cussed every now and again but he'll get over it."

Charlie grinned. "Flapjack it is, if that's alright with you. Your Mom must have been a Bible reader to name you Simon, with a last name like Peters you remind me of Simon Peter, Jesus' friend of the Bible."

Flapjack also grinned, a dribble of tobacco juice escaping from the lump in the side of his jaw and ran down to his chin, mixing with his beard stubble, where the back of his hand wiped it back to his mouth; "You guessed it and you watch out for that Toddy; He's been known to preach a sermon or two and not all of them with his tongue. Damn, opps, I mean dang; my steaks are burning. Gata go." He turned rather quickly for an old veteran and started for the cook fire on the run.

"Thanks, Flapjack. We'll be ready shortly." Charlie watched him go and noticed that the mood at the other fire had not improved. It was a camp divided and that was not good when you had to rely on the man next to you to save your life. Most seemed to side with the Sergeant and kept a respectful attitude around the Lieutenant but there were a few that were too friendly with the Lieutenant and were drawing hard looks from some of the more seasoned veterans in the group.

Charlie shrugged; he could not change this one so he did not think about it anymore. He went over to Ray and found her looking up at him from her blankets with a welcoming smile on her face. He signed that he would help her do her morning business and bent to lift her up. She placed a hand on his arm, stopping him and, speaking Delaware, said that she would like to try herself.

He signed OK, but he would lift her to her feet so that her wound would not tear and he bent and picked her up, gently placing her on her feet; then he held her waist to support her as they went down the wash.

Coming back, Charlie looked at the horses and was surprised to see the little mare herding with Joe, Nails and Molly; he thought "She seemed to like it better with us than the Indians." He got his canteen, when they got to camp, and poured a bowl full of water for Ray to wash up in. He had sat her on a pile of blankets and set the bowl on one of their packs. As she washed she started to hum and Charlie found that it was a very pleasant sound and that he enjoyed hearing it.

The sound soon drew the attention of the men in the camp and the mood seemed to lift a little with one or two of the soldiers starting to whistle along with her.

Flapjack arrived with a breakfast of steaks, beans and biscuits just as she got done and, when Charlie had thrown out the water, they said grace and dug in. Flapjack had brought them lots. They were nicely started when he again came over and brought them a large pot of coffee.

Ray tried some, but not before Charlie dug out some sugar that Flapjack had brought over and put a good amount in her coffee, first. After she tasted it, she made a sour face at him and grinned but she kept on drinking it.

"Darn kid is cute." Charlie mused before his attention was drawn to Arthur sitting at the other fire staring at them; at Ray really. Charlie had hoped that he would be over his infatuation this morning. Well, they would be leaving soon and that would be the end of it, Charlie hoped.

Breakfast finished, Charlie started putting the packs together. He had not gone through the dead men's saddlebags yet. He determined to do it in the near future; there might be something in them that Charlie would not want to get caught with. Thankfully the rest of their gear was in a pack that did not have to be opened. It might raise some questions to have extra guns, saddles and such truck with a man alone.

Ray sat on the blankets and, typical of the female sex, fussed with her hair and brushed her clothes; generally cleaning and tiding herself; as Charlie noted after a few minutes, making herself look darn pretty. Arthur was also paying a lot of attention to Ray and, it was obvious that his lust was getting a firm hold on him.

The troops had finished breakfast and were also getting ready to depart. Before they saddled their horses, Arthur came over to Charlie and Ray. His mood had still not changed and he snapped, "You seemed to be quite active last night. How did you get to Bill so fast and where did you go afterwards?" He was rude by western customs and he should have known better but Charlie decided not to push it.

"I heard the noise that Bill was making and went to investigate. I got there right after the Sergeant and, after we brought Bill back to camp, I went back to bed." He said; keeping his tone mild and inoffensive. He didn't lie; he just didn't tell Arthur where he was when he heard Bill.

"So, you know nothing about the Indian horses?" Arthur persisted.

"This morning I heard the Sergeant say something about the Indians and their horses. Why? What's wrong? Are my horses alright?" Charlie feinted concern.

"Your horses are there but the Indians broke into camp and stole theirs last night. There's going to be some sentries doing extra duty for letting them in, too. "

"I came here with twenty five horses and I consider them mine. Now you're telling me that some are missing. Those red thieves; if I didn't have this girl I'd go get my horses back." Charlie said this to try to ease the pressure against him that was coming from Arthur but, too late, he realized his mistake.

Arthur almost jumped, "We can look after the girl for you. We have lots of medical supplies and Flapjack is a fair good healer. You just go on and find your horses; she'll be alright." He was looking sideways at Ray as he finished.

"Oh, Lord; give me a boot, will you?" Charlie thought and he looked like he was thinking about it while he prayed for an answer to get out of this situation.

Just then, Ray fainted. She slumped to the side and rolled off the blankets; flopping in a heap on the ground. Both men jumped and ran to her. The rest of the soldiers, noticing what was happening, dropped what they were doing and ran to see if they could help.

Charlie got there first and, kneeling down, he gently rolled Ray over on her back. Then he grabbed his canteen and, wetting his bandana, wiped her mouth and face. Her eyes fluttered and opened but it took a while for them to focus on him. Charlie put a blanket under her head for support and to give it a soft place to rest. Seeing that she was alright, he stood up and, turning to Arthur, said, "Thanks for the offer but she needs to get to the doctor at the fort. She still has a ways to go to get better." In his heart he prayed, "Thanks, Lord."

Arthur scowled at him, then, after what seemed like a long time, he growled, "I have some more questions for you. You better stay around the fort until I get back. Don't leave or I will have to send my men after you." With that, he turned on his heel and strode away.

They heard him call as he got to the other fire, "Sergeant. Prepare the mounts."

As the soldiers moved to prepare their horses, Charlie rose and went to find Joe and the others. Joe was looking at him when he came in sight of the horses. Nails and the little mare whinnied and started towards him.

He was rubbing the mare's neck when Todd stepped up beside him. Deep in thought and preoccupied with his attention to his horses, Charlie had missed hearing him coming. He also took note that Todd could move very quietly when he wanted to. "He's giving you the right old go, isn't he?"

"Yes, He's got it in for Ray but he can't have her. I guess we'll cross that bridge when we get to it; right now she has got to mend." Charlie answered him.

"Yes, your right." Todd paused, "I would hate to lose my commanding officer, you know, and it would cause quite a stink for the one who done him in." The hint was obvious. When Charlie said nothing, Todd continued on another subject, "We're not going to find those Indians, are we?"

"No." Charlie grinned.

Todd grinned back, "Good. Well, have a good day and maybe I'll see you back at the fort soon."

On impulse, Charlie stuck out his hand and Todd grasped it in a firm handshake. They were developing a friendship and an understanding of each other that they both appreciated. Charlie figured that another good friend might be necessary before this was over, but he hoped it wouldn't come to anything.

Todd turned and moved towards his horse and Charlie gathered his herd and headed back to camp.

When he got there, Flapjack was sitting beside Ray telling her a story that she could not understand but, when he laughed, she smiled politely and nodded. He finished as Charlie came up and stood up. Sticking out his hand, he said, "Take good care of her, young fellow. She doesn't talk much but me and the boys have taken a shine to her."

Taking his hand, Charlie said, "Thanks, Flapjack; I'll do what I can. I'll see you at the fort."

"You can count on it." Flapjack said as he turned and hurried to his horse.

When the soldiers were ready to move out, Charlie watched them go and then saddled Nails. Again he put the travois on Joe and packs on Molly and the mare.

The soldiers were gone when they were ready. Ray was tucked in and Charlie mounted for the slow trip to Fort Benton.

As he rode, Charlie thought about their situation; he was the only thing keeping Arthur from getting Ray and poor little Ray was alone except for him to look out for her. Arthur wanted to keep them near the fort so he could get an opportunity to possess her; Charlie had to give her time to heal and then get her away as quickly as possible. If he had to kill Arthur, the Army would send its soldiers after him; he would not only be a fugitive from the law but would have Todd chasing him.

He decided that he could not hurt Todd; there was something about him that he liked. There had to be a way around this, but first things first, Ray had to have that time to heal.

He relaxed as much as a cautious man could; the Indians were now his friends and they would reach the fort early in the afternoon, at this pace.

He knew that God was in control and had a plan for their lives but Charlie wished that he had a little more insight as to what that plan was and what he was supposed to do with it.

The rain had not come and the sunshine was warm on his back; the grass was green from the moisture of two days ago and the horses' rhythm and horse sounds were comforting and relaxing.

Charlie felt glad to be here and started to hum a few bars of "In the Garden", but his eyes never stopped searching the surrounding countryside and he traveled with his guns loose in their holsters.

CHAPTER 7

They had traveled down the wash almost to its mouth, then cut across the plain. Topping the last rise before coming down to the fort, Charlie stopped. He had checked on Ray upon leaving the wash; giving her a drink of water and, when he checked her, found her pulse strong and her color was good but she had slept most of the way.

Now, he took a few minutes to look over the fort and the surrounding countryside.

Fort Benton had been built for defense; placed on a small knoll, having a good view of the surrounding country with only grass growing around it. There were trees for walls and houses along the Missouri River flowing a few miles to the south. They could also find rocks for fireplaces there.

The fort had a clear field of fire for five hundred yards in every direction around it. It had pole walls stood on end and sunk into the ground for strength and defense, and a guard tower in each corner that stuck out over the wall and gave the soldiers a field of gun fire close to the wall. Inside would be officers' quarters, bunkhouses for the soldiers, store houses, mess house, blacksmith shop, stables and doctors quarters/hospital, as one building. It would be as efficient and as well organized as an ant hill.

As with an older fort in a reasonably peaceful time, common citizens had started building outside the fort for trade with the Indians and to service the entertainment needs of the soldiers. On the southern edge of their field of fire, there was a general store, a couple of saloons, a hotel/eating house, a couple of dozen wood buildings housing some business', some families and some trappers and a number of tents and tepees of some less permanent residents.

Further away, over the rolling grassy plain, you could see what looked like three or four smaller settlements that were really cattle ranchers' headquarters built like mini-forts; made of wood and mud buildings put together for defense from the Indians.

In this part of the west at this time in history, this was as big a town as you would find for miles around. If the Indians acted up and tried to kill them, the town's people would go to the fort or the ranches and fight them off, usually. Now however, there were so many soldiers that the Indians were afraid to come too close to the community.

Charlie felt sure that Ray would be reasonably safe here. At least from the Indians; he wasn't so sure about the whites.

As they rode down the hill and across to the fort, Charlie was deciding his plan of action; first, see the army surgeon, then find a place to live for a few days. Getting closer, Charlie noticed what looked like a stable and, a cross on the top of one of the buildings suggested a church.

When they were within hailing distance of the fort, a soldier appeared on the catwalk and watched him as they came to the gate. He waited until they stopped in front of it before he spoke, "What can we do for you, Sir?"

The attitude here was one of reserved friendliness mixed with caution. That was a good sign, Charlie thought; meant that they had an experienced officer in charge and he run a good fort. Arthur probably had not been with them very long.

He answered the soldier, "Got a hurt girl here with me and I would like the surgeon to take a look at her." He waved towards the travois as he spoke. By now Charlie heard more soldiers moving on the other side of the gate.

The soldier on the wall hesitated a moment and then, glancing into the compound, spoke to someone that Charlie could not see. "Open the gate; two to come in."

Charlie started ahead and the gates opened as they reached them.

Once inside, Charlie saw that it was as he suspected; the fort was alive with soldiers all busy doing duty, repairing things and cleaning or washing uniforms and equipment. One soldier stepped out in front and waved for them to follow him while two more fell in behind them. They took them to what looked like a small bunkhouse. All the buildings backed onto the wall and faced a large open parade ground in the center of the fort. They had dug a well in the center of the parade ground with a wooden drinking trough beside it. There were hitching posts everywhere and many of the buildings had full front verandas that were scattered with projects of work for the day as well as drying clothes and benches.

Dismounting and giving Nail's reins a flip over the hitching post; he went to Joe and saw that Ray was awake. He signed that he was going to lift her out and not to be afraid, she would be alright. Her eyes had been looking around at the inside of the fort with a concerned, startled look but she smiled her trust and helped him part the blankets. Gently lifting her up, Charlie carried her to the door which opened as he got to it. He stopped just inside to let his eyes adjust to the different lighting and an older gentleman motioned for him to put the girl on a nearby bed; which he did.

"I'm the surgeon," he stated, "Where is she hurt and how can I help her?"

Charlie noted the crisp clean uniform and the well kept appearance of the surgeon and the well organized work place that he had as he replied, "She's taken a nasty knife wound to her lower back. I did the best I could for her with what I had but I would appreciate your looking at her, Sir."

"By all means, young man; could we get her rolled over and her shirt up a little?"

They rolled Ray over and she laid still as the doctor examined her; moving her skin here and there and pressing one place or another. The doctor was slightly shorter than Charlie with hair graying at the temples. He was slight of form but his hands were sure and steady; moving easily with no wasted motions.

After ten minutes, he straightened, going to a cupboard, he brought back a bottle of liquid and, putting some on a cloth, bathed the whole wound with it. Then he got a clean pad and wrapped the wound with a fresh bandage. He did not speak until they had Ray rolled over on her back again, "She should rest for a few more days and then be careful not to move around quickly or she could tear her wound open again. If you like, she can stay here; as you can see, we are not very busy and have the room. It would be cleaner than any place in town. You did a very good job with that stitching." He added, eyeing Charlie carefully.

He was hinting at an explanation for Charlie's skills but Charlie disappointed him. "That would be right nice of you and we accept only if I can bunk fairly close. I'm kind of fond of her, Sir." He added to cover more questions.

"Of course and it is Major Bob Stewart; Sir is for soldiers not civilians. One of our men, Sergeant Todd McKinley, has his wife and children here at the fort with him and she doubles as the fort's nurse. She will take good care of your girl."

"I've met the Sergeant, Major, and he strikes me as a stand up guy. My name is Charlie and, if it will not offend you, I can pay for your services and housing."

"That would offend me greatly, Charlie, so we will not hear any more about that. The Army pays me quite enough and they also provide the housing. Now," turning to one of the soldiers who had waited by the door, he spoke "Bennett, bunk this man next door in the bunkhouse and show him where he can put his horses. I'll inform the Colonel that he is here."

Charlie took a few minutes, when Bob left, to explain to Ray what they were doing. Using sign and Delaware he made sure that she was at ease with the situation and then he followed Bennett. It was obvious that Bennett was cavalry when outside the door, instead of turning left towards the bunkhouse; he immediately turned and followed Charlie to the horses. He led the way to the stables which were almost straight across from the bunkhouse and helped Charlie care for his horses; rubbing them down and giving them a little grain as a treat.

Charlie found an empty stall and stored his packs and gear in it; taking just what he and Ray would need.

The bunkhouse was back across the parade ground, beside the surgeon's quarters where he would be close to Ray. When they entered the building, Charlie saw that it was long with a row of bunk beds, headfirst against each wall and had a narrow isle in the middle between them. Bennett kept leading him to the near corner against the wall that separated the bunkhouse from the hospital, to an empty upper bunk. It would be stifling hot in the upper bunk but he thanked Bennett because he could see that he had taken him to the nearest available point to Ray that he could. By the time he had set his blankets and personal items on his bunk, it was almost supper time. He could look around later, he had things that he wanted to do and the time was slipping by quickly; he had to make sure that Ray was looked after so he could leave.

He found her sitting up against a stack of pillows and talking in sign language to a strikingly pretty lady. Her cameo face was framed by raven, black hair; heavily built but not plump and when Charlie noticed her work worn hands, he knew why. She stood up and turned towards him, as Charlie entered the room and he could see that she was quite tall. She had a quiet, confident air about her. "Can I help you?" She asked. Her voice was husky but not unpleasant; giving the impression of being older and more mature than her looks suggested.

There were, also, two children sitting on the next bed; a boy, about four years old, and a girl, about seven. By the common features they shared with the woman, it was obvious that they were her children. The little girl's mouth was a mirror of her mothers and the boy had the same serious and direct look in his blue eyes as his mother. Their hair had just a hint of red and was lighter than their mothers, leading Charlie to believe that the red tint came from one Sergeant Todd McKinley. They had been watching the sign language and now stared at this dirty rough man standing before them.

Charlie, always a lover of children, grinned and winked at them. He was rewarded with two smiles and a titter from the girl. Their mother smiled and waited.

Ray tugged at the lady's sleeve and, when she looked down at Ray; Ray signed that this was her man. Charlie kept his troubling thoughts about her possessiveness to himself and said, "I'm the one that found her on the prairie and brought her here. My name is Charlie Power, ma'am."

The lady paused and thought awhile, then said, "I'm Ruth McKinley and I'm pleased to meet you. Please, forgive my silence but I think that I have heard that name before; I just can't remember where right now." Waving her hand towards the children she continued, "These are my children; Beth and Carl. Children, say hello to Mister Power."

"Hello, Sir." They chimed together; looking very serious.

"Hi," he replied, with a wave and another smile. Looking at Ruth, he said, "I hope when you remember where you heard my name before, it was in a good circumstance." She didn't reply and Charlie continued, "You're the nurse that the Major told me about?"

"I'm not a nurse but I've learned quite a bit about helping the sick and the wounded from the Major and he gets me to help out whenever he needs me to." She replied.

"Could you look after Ray tonight, please? I have a job that needs to be done and I might not be back until morning."

A strange look flitted across her face as she answered, "Yes, I can do that. You will be back, Mr. Power?" It was asked like a question but there was an iron command in her voice and her countenance noticeably darkened.

"Yes, ma'am; I was told to stay around by Arthur" she wrinkled her nose in distaste "and I met a guy named 'Todd' that I would like to see again." At the mention of her husband, her face took on a new glow and see looked at Charlie a little sharper. Charlie knew he had eased her fears that he would run away and he walked over and sat down by Ray. With sign and Delaware, he explained to her that Ruth would look after her tonight and that he had some business to look after and that he should be back for breakfast in the morning. She never doubted him but nodded her assent and smiled at him.

Ruth said, "Go get some supper, Charlie; I'll tend to her."

Before Charlie got up to leave, he poked the boy gently in the ribs and winked at Beth again. They both laughed the boy, Carl, happily holding his stomach and almost as one person chimed a merry "good-bye".

Charlie immediately went to the stable and saddled Joe; then taking the Indian mare with two of the extra saddles, one of the spare rifles and half a box of shells, he left the fort in the direction of town. He ate some jerky as he rode, making some quick plans and a list of things to get.

The town was larger than he had seen coming in over the plain with more, smaller buildings between the larger ones. Its one main street was crossed a couple of times by two side streets that each ended into open prairie after a few houses. The businesses were mostly in the center block but there was a stable just where he entered on the edge of town; a lean-to, one room house was attached to the side of it and, out back, was a scattering of corrals and small outbuildings.

He stopped first at the stable and, finding it empty, he passed through the two big open doors at each end following the sound of horses being worked out back. In the center of a dusty horse corral, he could see a giant of a man leading a two year old horse around with a half-full oat bag on its saddle. He was getting it used to a weighted saddle so that it could be ridden and not be alarmed at the weight on its back.

Charlie watched through the gate as the man talked to the horse while he worked with it. He noticed that he gently moved the horse where he wanted it to go; talking in a low steady voice all the while. Charlie had seen few men 'gentle' a wild horse. Most got on its back and rode it until it stopped fighting. The horse would give up sooner or later but it would take a lot of the horse's spirit out, too; leaving it just another dumb animal to be led around on a lead rope. By gentling a horse, you left it its spirit and made it your friend so it wanted to do what you asked of it. The young sorrel gelding was listening to the man, its ears moving back and forth as he talked.

The man finally noticed Charlie and brought the horse over to the gate. He moved very easily for such a big man; rolling on the balls of his feet and carrying his great weight with the ease of a very strong man. Dressed in jeans and an open front leather vest, he also had on a leather apron covered with the marks of hot metal splashed on it from his blacksmith's hammer. His huge bare chest covered with black hair, matching his close cropped head hair; a bandana tied around his head kept his sweat out of his eyes.

"Yes, Sir, what can I help you with?" As he talked he continued to rub the horse's ear.

Charlie hid his surprise at the man's politeness and looked at him. He stood almost seven feet tall and must have weighed two hundred and eighty pounds or better. His hands were calloused and rough and the black hair on his arms couldn't hide the bulging work hardened muscles. He had on homemade cowhide boots held together with strips of rawhide because his feet were so big. The rawhide must have been sewn in wet because it had shrunk and pulled the edges of the boots tight; making them almost waterproof. Someone had a head for sewing and making clothes because it was a real good job. Charlie looked at his face and saw that his features were clean and chunky but he had soft brown eyes and a mouth that was quick to smile.

Charlie found himself liking this gentle giant right away.

"I'd like to buy a good horse, if you've got one to sell." He said

"Yes, Sir; we have three in that corral," and he turned and waved to three horses looking at them over another corral fence to Charlie's right. A boy of about eight came around the corral fence just then and started towards them. He was also built like his father but with lighter hair. Dressed in one-piece bib-overalls that he had almost outgrown, floppy ten-gallon hat that was a size too big and bare feet he was moving quickly towards the men, intent on satisfying his curiosity about Charlie.

The men were watching him come towards them when they heard a rattle like pebbles in a dry leather pouch. The giant froze and the boy stopped; looking down, his complexion paled. Coiled beside a rock, sunning itself was a diamond back rattlesnake within three feet of the boy. The men had not seen it behind the rock but now could see its head and neck as it rose to strike.

"Dad?" the boy whispered and the man sighed and a choking sound started deep in his chest.

Time stood still as the snake opened its mouth and lunged at the boy's calf.

The giant was reaching for the top rail of the corral to climb over it and Charlie, standing a couple of steps from it, had half-turned towards the boy as he watched him approach.

Charlie's hands were a blur as he drew and fired both guns simultaneously and, through the gun-smoke, he saw the snakes head explode in a red splash of blood; the lifeless body continuing on to strike the boy harmlessly in the leg; leaving a large red splotch of the snake's blood on the boy's overalls.

The boy watched in stunned silence as the headless body coiled and recoiled itself on the ground. The giant lifted a shaking hand to his face and wiped the sweat, which had instantly appeared there, away. He came over the corral fence and ran to the boy; scooping him up in his arms he looked all over him, making sure that he was alright. Charlie followed a few steps behind him, not wanting to interfere with the giant's scrutiny of his son.

Unashamed, he turned with the boy still in his arms and looked at Charlie. With tears starting down his face, his voice was almost a whisper as he said, "Sir, I owe you my life. This is my only child. If there is any way that I can repay you for what you have done, you just have to name it."

Taken back, Charlie was almost overwhelmed by the pure, raw emotion he saw in the man's face. "I could do nothing else," he said, "My reaction was pure instinct. I couldn't stand by and see the boy die while I could possibly do something to prevent it."

Just then two men came running out the back of the stable and, spying the giant standing with his son, started asking questions about the gunshots; suspiciously eyeing Charlie and his guns, which he had put away after reloading them. They were towns people dressed in city pants and shirts and more people could be heard coming through the stable.

"It's alright," the giant said, "Just a snake that tried to bite my Sam and this man shot it. It's alright; go on back." He set his son down, embarrassed that so many people were gathering around and making him the center of attention.

Charlie noticed that, even though his emotions were deep and strong, this was a very humble man and not used to being the center of attention as the crowd swelled to almost forty people.

The crowd finally dispersed with sidelong glances at Charlie, accepting the giant's explanation but, after looking at the headless snake's body and at Charlie's gun rigging, he could hear the murmurs and see the talking going on behind their hand-covered mouths as they glanced at Charlie and his guns; speculating about the speed and accuracy of his six guns. They were openly curious but fear held them from looking straight at or talking to him.

The giant followed the last man to the stable door and, as he went through it, turned back to Charlie.

"Sir, how can I thank you; what can I do to repay you?" He had regained his quiet nature again but was still inwardly shaken. Sam had come up to within a few paces of Charlie and was openly looking at him and his guns.

Charlie said, "Well, I need to buy a horse and I have two saddles that I don't need."

The giant studied his face for a few minutes, then, "Yes, I have those three that I was pointing to; you can take your pick. I've handled all three of them and any one of them would make you a good horse." He hesitated, then, "Not to be nosy or anything but could you tell me your name, please?"

The boy, Sam, had fallen into step behind them as they walked to the far corral and Charlie could feel his eyes continuing to studying him.

"You can call me Charlie." He said, "And you don't owe me anything mister…?"

"Smith, Tim Smith and this is my boy, Sam. He's our only child; my wife, Susan, and me came west last fall and settled here. I been working here to feed them. I hope that you are going to stay around for awhile, 'cause Susan will want to thank you."

"Yes, I've got a hurt girl to look after and we'll be here for a few days." They had reached the corral and Charlie could see that the horses were in good shape. Looking them over, he chose a big brown gelding and asked the price.

"Shifty's been asking a hundred dollars for that one, Charlie. He's the owner and he gets mad as all get out if I don't get his prices for him." Tim confided, embarrassed.

"Ok," Charlie said, "Look at the saddles and tell me what they're worth to you and we'll talk."

Tim put a lead rope on the horse and they took him with them back to the front of the stable. By now Sam was getting a little bolder and said, "Mr. Charlie, thanks for killing that snake. Could you show me how to shoot like that?"

Charlie stopped and looked at Sam. Not seeing any malice or bravado but only open honesty he said, "Your welcome, Sam and, please, call me Charlie. Probably not, son, shooting like that takes time to learn and lots of practice. Every man handles a gun differently and there is a comfortable and easy way for you to handle one, too. Only you will know that way when you try it. I could give you tips and advice, though, but only if your Mom and Dad say that it is OK."

"We won't bother Charlie with that right now Sam," Tim said and, when he saw Sam's face fall in disappointment, Charlie added, "Yes, Sam, you haven't talked to your Mom about it yet. You talk to your parents and get their permission then you come see me."

Sam brightened with Charlie's words and they continued on to look at the two saddles. After looking them over, Tim told Charlie that Shifty would probably only allow him twenty dollars apiece for them.

Charlie knew that this Shifty was a hard person to deal with but he was in a hurry and he liked Tim and Sam so he agreed. He paid for the horse and Tim made him out a bill-of-sale then they shook hands receiving an open invitation to come to Tim's home for a meal when he had the chance and meet Susan.

After shaking Tim's hand, Charlie turned, without a word, and stuck his hand out to Sam for a man sized handshake and knew instantly that he had done the right thing. Sam, realizing that Charlie was treating him like a man, straightened his shoulders and lifted his head to look in his eyes, and then he took Charlie's offered hand and gave him a firm handshake.

Charlie believed that he had made friends with two good men just now as he turned to leave.

Taking his herd and waving goodbye, he went to the general store, in the middle of the next block, and bought a pack and supplies to put on the horse. The supplies included food; 20 lbs of sugar, 20 lbs of salt and 50 lbs of cornmeal, a dozen good knives, two more boxes of bullets and a couple of bullet belts, a large bag of candy, a 10 lb bag of colored beads, six axes and four large hanging cooking pots. The store clerk, a young man, kept glancing at Charlie from the corner of his eyes as he filled out Charlie's order. He had been one of those that had been to the back of the stable after the shooting and was curious about him.

It took him some time to load everything onto the pack that he had kept and had transferred from the mare to the new gelding. Mounting Joe and with the lead ropes of the mare and the new horses tied to his saddle-horn he started for the river; another mile past the town. By this time, the sun was starting to set. He could see and feel the eyes of the towns' people on him as he made his way through the town and he knew that he would be the news hit of the night for the local gossipers.

He arrived at the river in the twilight and, stripping off his clothes, took a good bath. He shaved by feel and put on a clean shirt; then he sat down to wait.

He done some talking to God and some planning for the next couple of days. He was not looking forward to Arthur coming back while he and Ray were still there, but he did not want the Army chasing him either. The Major looked like a competent healer and would be a great help and he was pleased that Ruth could communicate with Ray and share her attention.

He had left his horse saddled and ready and, along about twelve o'clock, he heard the swish of movement in the water. Mounting Joe, he waited in the shadow of the trees at the water's edge. In another moment, out of the night came a movement down the river; shadows emerged and became horsemen; traveling single file, in the water and about ten or twelve feet from the bank. He held his horses from whinnying and, when the figures were opposite him, he spoke quietly in Sioux, "My friend, Great Bear; do you have a moment to talk?"

In true Indian fashion, everyone stopped and was completely still. Their surprise was complete; this was the last thing that they had expected. Finally a voice from the group asked, "Who can best an Indian in silence and stealth and catch him who can move like a shadow? Talking Fire Hand, my friend, it is good to hear your voice."

Charlie answered him, "Do not leave the water, for you are wise to hide your trail. I will come to you." And he rode out of the shadows, into the river to them. When he reached Great Bear he signed the Indian welcome and then held out his hand to grasp the hand of his friend in a white-man's handshake. Capturing Ray and killing her party was the Indian way of life and war; normal for them; Charlie found that Great Bear did not begrudge him taking Ray but, rather, thought it quite normal to be bested in fair combat by a superior warrior. He did not envy or hate Charlie, but thought it a privilege to be his friend.

As with Indian customs, they made small talk, asking each others health and the wellness of their families. They talked of the night and the trip that the Indians were making. Charlie learned a lot, just in the small talk.

He found out that the reason the Indians were so busy that night at the river was because the young bucks wanted to raid in the area, while they were looking for Ray, but Great Bear and the elders of his party thought that them not finding Ray was a bad omen and they wanted to leave the area without her. It had turned into a heated discussion and only ended when they found their horses gone. That's when the young men decided to agree with the older ones that this was bad country and that the gods were angry with them.

Charlie silently thanked God for His protection by this strange discussion and Great Bear confirmed that God was not happy with them when they were knocked out by Talking Fire Hand and that, when Talking Fire Hand helped them it drove the evil spirit from them and by doing what Talking Fire Hand had told them to do, they were confident that God was now pleased with them and that they would be fine.

Great Bear went into great detail about the army's search for them and how they eluded them with ease and how the army seemed to be distracted by an ambush site that they came upon. Great Bear's braves had also seen this site and the destruction that one man had caused three other men. Charlie could feel his words searching for Charlie's response when Great Bear suggested that such destruction could only be caused by a great warrior like himself, Talking Fire Hand.

He reminded Great Bear that God does some things that he does not want others to know about and Great bear grunted his assent to that wisdom.

After an hour, Charlie could get to the business he had come for and, when he found out that the mare, because she wanted to stay with him, became a gift from the Indians, he presented his gift of the horse and pack to the tribe. After they had accepted, with much surprise and happiness, he pulled out the rifle, still in its scabbard and presented it, the bullets and the bullet belts to Great Bear. Great Bear held the rifle aloft for the whole tribe to see and shook it, his face spread with a huge smile. The braves hooted and grunted their approval and the squaws clucked their tongues and raised their hand in appreciation. They were careful to keep the noise low so that they would not be heard if anyone were close by.

Then he presented to each Indian one of the knives. There was much murmuring among the Indians because they had never encountered a white man that gave them gifts in friendship, not asking for anything in return. Charlie had succeeded in making them his friends and, as they departed down the river and as each one passed him, he grasped their hand and said in Sioux, "May the Great Spirit be with you, my friend."

When they were out of sight, Charlie turned and headed back to the town; skirting around it so he would not draw attention, he stopped just past it, in a grassy dip and dismounting, he unsaddled his horses and rolled up in his blankets, he went to sleep. He left Joe and the Mare loose to graze and relax; trusting Joe to warn him of any danger and to look after the mare, Charlie knew that Joe would not go far from him.

CHAPTER 8

He was up again and just reaching the fort gates when reveille began sounding inside the fort. The morning guard saw him coming and opened the gates; he supposed that everyone knew that they were here, now. Nothing remains a secret for long in a small close community like a fort or a town.

The Indian mare followed behind Joe without a lead rope. She was a pinto; large black and brown spots with some white mixed in around them commonly called a paint. She was a pretty horse and very friendly so Charlie decided to give her to Ray. He unsaddled Joe and put the horses in the stable; patting Molly and Nails as he worked around them. Nails seemed a little upset that he had been left behind but soon got over it when Charlie scratched his neck and rubbed his head; he leaned his head on Charlie's shoulder and rolled his eyes back in his head, relishing every little scratch under his chin.

His next stop was the hospital, where he found Ray half sitting up leaning on some pillows and feeding herself from a plate of food.

Ruth was there, having brought Ray her breakfast and helped her with her morning necessities. Beth and Carl were there also eating their meal at the table. Ray's face lit up when she saw Charlie but Ruth spoke first, "You kept your word, that's good. The children have taken a liking to Ray and insisted on having breakfast with her; Beth even led in saying grace."

"Good girl," Charlie praised her and he could see the red start from her neck and creep onto her checks but she sat up a little straighter, liking the praise from this man. Carl, not to be outdone, said, "Me said it, too," and was quickly corrected by his mother, "I said it, too."

Charlie grinned and said, "Me glad you did, little man." That brought a scowl from Ruth but he knew they liked his answer when the kids tittered and Ray and Ruth smiled.

Sobering for a while, he said, "If you don't need me for anything, I'll go see what this Army food can do about filling this hole in my stomach," and he signed the same to Ray. Ruth and Ray both shook their heads, no, so he turned and left.

He entered into the mess hall and, out of habit, sidestepped to his left. He had been thinking of the dangers that they had been in and had done this side-step purely without realizing that he was safe at the fort. Most men holding a gun and waiting to shoot a man are right handed and their first instinct is to pull to the inside or their left. It takes a few precious seconds to realize their mistake and correct their aim when their target moves in a direction that they are not expecting; seconds that would give Charlie's eyes time to adjust to the low lighting, draw and fire. Too late, he realized that he had just told everyone in the room that he was no stranger to trouble and that he lived because others had died. They would expect this action from an older gunfighter, not a young man of twenty two. Charlie tried to cover his action by moving quickly into the room and, only recognizing the Major, moved to sit beside him. He was fortunate that there was an empty plate there. Even though there were twenty men on Arthur's patrol, the room was almost full and Charlie drew more than a passing glance from most of them. They had heard about Ray and the Sioux and their imaginations made Charlie out to be some kind of deadly Indian fighter.

The room was long and narrow, holding three long tables with bench seats on both sides of them. At the end of the room was a doorway through which Charlie could see the cook and his helper cleaning up after cooking the huge meal. The tables were loaded down with bowls and platters of food.

As he reached the Major, Charlie realized that he had to get his own plate and utensils and continued on past Bob nodding his recognition as he passed. He studied the soldiers as he retrieved the things he needed, looking for anyone that he might know but they were all strangers to him.

Nodding again to the Major, he started to fill his plate from the bowls of eggs, beans, corn, steak and bread that were on the table. While he worked, he talked to the Major, "Good morning, Major, I want to thank you for taking us in like that and for looking after Ray."

"Ray? Oh yes, the girl. You're welcome, Charlie."

In a lower tone that only carried to the Major, Charlie said, "I also appreciated that you did not hesitate to treat her any different because she's an Indian."

Major Stewart raised his eyebrows and said, "She is a hurt human being and that's who I am trained to help. Some people, and even some here, do not think that way but I don't share their opinion." He did not lower his voice when he spoke and a number of soldiers turned their heads to look at them, some with angry looks on their faces.

Like the patrol, this fort was divided in its opinions also.

Changing the subject, he said, "The Colonel would like to see you, when you get a minute." He paused and then continued, "You did a very professional looking job of sewing that wound together." He left the sentence hanging, again trying to get a little more information.

Charlie gave him a little, "My Dad taught me a lot about helping hurt people. He taught from God's good book to everybody he met, then, helped them with their needs. A lot had physical needs and

Dad, wanting to help as best he could, learned about healing. He would tell me, "You can't help someone, if you don't know how.""

"Good advice." Bob said thoughtfully. "Sounds like a man I once knew back in Washington. He has the same name as you, too. He was always telling people about God and the Bible and, even, about how to do things the right way. He and Mister Lincoln would meet regularly and talk right and wrong, they tell me. They say he was well off but he and his wife, Betty, I think, lived in a poor part of town in a simple townhouse. People that knew them said that their word was always good no matter what they said. It's also said that he was Mister Lincoln's unofficial Indian adviser. They say that he was also advising Mister Johnson and, now that Ulysses Grant is President, things might change." He continued, "I haven't met the man, myself, but he is known by his reputation in some very powerful groups back east."

Charlie swallowed hard. He was talking about Charlie's Dad. Charlie was named for his Dad but, instead of calling him Charlie junior, he was known as Chuck by his parents; a nickname his mother gave him when he was very young so she could call them differently. He decided to keep his last name a secret if he could get Ruth McKinley not to tell anyone. Powerful people also have their enemies; possibly even out here.

"Sounds like a man worth knowing," Charlie said and, to change the subject, "What is the Colonel's name?"

"Colonel Leonard Belmont, he's been with us about six years now. An old war horse from Massachusetts; his son just got a transfer here last spring and Leonard is some proud. He's Army all the way and was some pleased when his son followed; he's a lieutenant here."

Charlie wanted to swear again but knew that that was not the Christian way. God had a way out of this; he just had to find it.

Major Stewart continued, "I'll introduce you, if you like; right now I had better leave you alone to eat. You haven't touched your breakfast and its getting cold. I'll see you later." He got up and joined another officer as he was leaving.

Some of the remaining soldiers were still watching Charlie but he didn't care, he bowed his head and prayed for his food. Then he took a few minutes to see if the Lord had any answers for this situation he was in. He drew a blank, "Well, Lord, I guess I go on faith then. I know you're there and you have a plan but, darn it, could you give me a hint at least?" He concluded that God had His time and that was that so Charlie dug into his now cold food and stopped worrying about what might happen.

Having satisfied his hunger, Charlie went first to the hospital to see if he could find Mrs. McKinley. He almost ran into her as he stepped into the room. "Oh!" she exclaimed; coming to a full stop. "Washington, DC; you look just like him."

Instantly Charlie shushed her and said, "Please, don't tell on me. These people don't know my last name and I have reason for them not to know me." And Charlie told her about Arthur's infatuation with Ray and the trouble that might be looming in the near future. He had already told her his name; now he had to trust her but, being Todd's wife, he figured he could.

Different expressions crossed her face as he talked until, finally, he stopped. She had settled on a serious and firm expression that she explained in two words, "That snake!" After a slight pause, she continued, "This poor little thing can't be more than fifteen. He'll get her over my dead body." Her chin raised a little as she talked and Charlie knew that Arthur was in for a rough ride if he tried anything with Ray while she was around.

"You had better hang around, Charlie; the Colonel thinks a lot of his son and, if he ordered you to stay, his father will back him up and I won't tell anyone your last name but it won't be a secret long. There are a lot of folks from Washington here and your Dad is well known to them. Bob; the Major can also be trusted. He may be Army through and through but he's a Christian and faithful, just don't put him in a position to have to choose between the two."

The two children had sensed the seriousness of the situation and had stayed back by Ray, who lay watching them. Now they ran forward and hung on to Ruth's dress; peeking around it at Charlie. He rewarded them with a surprised look and a wink. He bent down and asked, "Have you been looking after Ray while I was out?" They both nodded and Beth said, "Uhah, and she's going to get weller." "Better." Ruth corrected.

Carl said, "Raeeee, patted my head real soft. She's nice."

Ruth shooed them out saying, "Its time for your schooling, now. You can come visit later." And they headed for the door but, before they left, Ruth turned and gave Charlie a serious but supportive look; giving her head a nod, she turned and went out, following her children.

He spent some time telling Ray what the Major and Ruth had said and about his new friends, the Sioux. She seemed glad to finally not to have to worry about the Indians anymore and told Charlie that she trusted him and whatever he decided to do, they would do and he would make it alright. During the conversation, she found opportunity to touch his hand a few times; gently, caressingly; showing an intimate possessiveness that disturbed Charlie.

The promise of rain that Charlie noticed yesterday morning came with a wind gust and a sudden downpour. It rained hard for awhile, then settled in for a long steady drizzle. Charlie knew that Great Bear and his band had gotten away and he wondered how long Arthur would keep his soldiers out looking for them. He hoped, long enough for Ray to get well enough to move to town. Here at the fort, Arthur would have easy access to her in spite of Charlie and Ruth.

Charlie lay down in one of the spare beds within sight of Ray, who was dozing, and caught a nap. He was awakened by the door opening to let Major Stewart in just before noon. The major shook the rain from his hat and looked at Charlie; amusement in his eyes. He didn't say anything but watched as Charlie put his gun away; not having remembered drawing it. "Sorry, I guess I might be a little nervous." He said.

"No need to apologize, my boy. I've seen those that have lived with trouble and those that have died because of it." He paused and looked pointedly at Charlie, "You're still alive." As he walked to his desk he continued, "The Colonel would like to meet you over at the mess hall and have dinner with you, if you like."

"Sure." Charlie responded; sitting up and stretching his arms.

"Ruth and the kids will be in shortly with dinner for Ray and I'll take a look at her wound this afternoon. Those kids have fallen in love with her; she's all they can talk about." Bob continued, "Whenever you're ready, I'll take you over and introduce you to the Colonel."

Charlie told Ray that Ruth and the kids would be in soon and that he would be back after lunch, then he and Bob trudged through the water soaked parade grounds to the mess hall, where they went inside. As before, the three long tables were almost filled with food; active people need to eat and obviously the Colonel kept his men busy. Bowls of food were rowed in the center of each table and the soldiers were digging in to dinner. The tables were almost full but, along the right outside row and beside a big, heavy-set man in a Colonel's uniform, there were two open places. After collecting their plate and utensils, Bob took Charlie to them and sat down beside the Colonel, placing himself between the two; almost as if he knew that this meeting might not go all that well.

Bob spoke first, "Colonel, this is the man that came in last night. Charlie, meet Colonel Leonard Belmont."

"Colonel, glad to meet you and thank you for your hospitality; it's appreciated." Charlie said. He did not hold out his hand as the Colonel did not get up or reach to welcome him but sat there regarding him coolly for a few seconds. He was an imposing man with large features; not overly tall but everything else seemed large; head, nose, mouth, eyes, hands. Everything that Charlie saw seemed too big for his body; even his long, handle-bar mustache seemed too large for his lip and showed many grey hairs mixed with his natural sand colored hair. His eyes bulged and were bloodshot and his nose was red tipped reminding Charlie of some of the older miners that tended to drink just a little too much but, with the Colonel, who he had just met, it was too early for him to know for sure. The Colonel might spend a lot of late nights working at writing reports or such things. The Colonel was an older and heavier Arthur with the same hair color and style, same jutting chin and glaring eyes.

"You look familiar," Colonel Belmont finally said, "like someone I should know but I don't think I've ever met you." His voice was like his features, deep and booming.

"No," Said Charlie, "We've never met." The Major sat down and beckoned for Charlie to sit beside him. "He's had a time with a hurt girl and dodging the Sioux; could probably use a day or two's rest. I'm looking at the girl later but she shouldn't be moved for awhile. Dig in Charlie." He said as he filled his plate.

The Colonel eyed Charlie as he ate but didn't say anything. Charlie could almost feel his eyes as they traveled over his muscular shoulders and arms and down to his waist; taking in his unusual gun rigging and knife handle. When Bob had filled his plate, he bowed his head and said grace. The Colonel grunted in disgust but Charlie instinctively bowed his head also.

When Bob was done, the Colonel said, "So your one of them, are you?"

"If you mean a Christian, yes; I know and serve Jesus the messiah," Said Charlie, looking the Colonel square in the eyes having met opposition like this before. The Colonel grunted again but changed the subject, "Where did you find this girl and what happened to her."

"Out on the plain, unconscious, on a rock and she had been knifed by an Indian," he said, not wanting to give the Colonel much detail and leaving out all about the three dead men. "I helped her and hid her, and then we found our way here."

The Colonel frowned, noticing the lack of detail in the simple explanation. It was obvious that he wanted more but western tradition counted it rude to push a man for information and question his past. As red anger color started to slowly work its way from the Colonel's neck upward, the Major quietly said, "Charlie is used to trouble, Leonard" using his first name hoping to ease the tension, "he brought her through the Sioux and handles himself like a fighter. Being a civilian, he might have a few things in his past that he doesn't want talked about." The implication was obvious and would not have made a difference to the Colonel, surrounded by his men, but the mention that he was a civilian stopped him.

Changing the subject, the Colonel said, "There was some shooting in town, last night; you know anything about that?" He stared accusingly at Charlie as he spoke.

Charlie shrugged and, speaking around his food, told him about the shooting of the snake; making it sound like it was a lucky shot and not his usual accuracy.

The Colonel volunteered, "The townies are saying that it was some mighty fancy shooting; some mighty *accurate* shooting." And his eyes drilled into Charlie's, searching for answers.

Charlie shrugged, "I had to try and it worked, I couldn't just let the boy get bit. I'm thankful that I didn't hit him."

"You seem to have a knack for helping people; first, the girl and now this Smith brat." The Colonel sneered.

"Leonard, ease up a little. Charlie is new around here and fell into trouble right from the get-go." The Major said, speaking softly.

Charlie put another spoonful of food in his mouth to hide his surprise. He hadn't known that the Colonel had been in to see Ray and didn't know where his animosity was coming from. He chewed his food slowly, saying nothing.

Colonel Belmont stared hard at him for a long time, then got up and left without a parting word; his energy and drive evident in the force of the push from the table and the hard stamp of his boots and swing of his arms as he walked.

"Thanks," Charlie whispered, after he left.

"Your welcome," Bob answered, "I've known him for a long time now; he's a good soldier and knows how to fight and win but he has a bad streak that comes out now and again."

They talked through the rest of their meal and Charlie found himself liking this quiet surgeon. The Major had an English military background and training and was posted in this out-of-the-way fort because of the things he had spoken out against in Washington. He had run afoul of some very powerful political people who had wanted him out of the way.

Their meal over, Charlie and Bob went back to the hospital were they found Ray surrounded by Ruth and the kids. They had eaten and the kids were trying to teach Ray to speak in English; holding up objects and telling her what they were. They were having so much fun that the men hated to interrupt them. Their laughter was infectious and they were all soon laughing at the sounds the kids and Ray were making.

Finally, Bob, seeing that Ray was getting tired, called a halt to the game, saying that he had to look at her wound. Ruth was going to take the kids out but the Major said that they could stay, if they wanted to because they would not see anything that they shouldn't and might learn a little about healing. Ruth frowned at the Major but the kids were allowed to stay, much to their delight.

Charlie gently rolled Ray over and they lifted her shirt, just enough to see the wound. When they removed the bandages, they saw that it was pink and healing; the stitches were still good and the wound was not open or running fluid. Bob cleaned the skin around the wound again and disinfected the area then bandaged it again with a clean bandage.

"A few more days and we can take the stitches out," he said. "We have a chair here that we put some wheels on. If you like she can use it tomorrow and we can move her around a little; maybe outside, if it stops raining."

"Yaa," both kids chimed at the same time, "Can we push it?"

"Better ask your mom and Charlie," Bob said with a grin.

"Maybe," Charlie said, taking the responsibility for saying no away from Ruth. She smiled her thanks and Charlie frowned at Bob for setting them up with the kids like that. Bob shrugged and pretended to be sheepish and repentant which they all laughed at.

Bob, ever busy somewhere, stated that he had to be at another part of the fort but Charlie suspected that he was giving the hint for everyone to leave and let Ray rest. Ruth took the hint and shooed the two kids out "for more schooling" she said.

After everybody had left, Charlie signed for Ray to rest and he went out to the stable. He fed and rubbed the horses, taking his time and talking softly to each one in turn; then sat down to look through the dead men's saddlebags and packs. Of the three extra saddles, he had traded the two larger ones and kept the small one; he would give that to Ray. He also kept her the best bridle and hung the other two on some nails in the stable; the Army could always use some spares. The saddle blankets he kept; they could always be used for sleeping blankets. One rifle he had given to Great Bear, the other two he wrapped in their scabbards with some ammunition; these he would give to some poor farmer or someone to help them get game to eat. He did the same with the three extra hand guns and holster belts.

Before he put each gun away, he broke it open, oiled it, worked the hammer and made sure that it worked smoothly.

The stable was a large single room and, much like the bunkhouse, had two rows of horse stalls running through the middle from one end to the other, left and right from the door and they were almost full of horses. The horse sounds and the rain outside made a steady, relaxing noise and he did not hear the footsteps behind him. He had the last of the guns in his hand; it was a 38 special that was very well balanced. A 38 was a small caliber and was rare in this wilderness; it was considered a lady's gun. He checked the balance again with a roll of his hand then, in a flash, he spun the gun on his index finger, holstered it and drew it, spun it on his finger again; changing hands while it was spinning, stopping it holding the barrel and then done a Texas border roll. The gun seemed to flash and dance like it had a life of its own and it had hardly stopped when he heard a gasp behind him; he spun with the gun ready for business, eyes searching for the maker of the noise. He had deliberately picked a dark corner of the stable so that the packs would not be disturbed and he could go through them unnoticed. He was not expecting anyone to be around so he expected the worst.

There, standing just behind and half hidden by the last horse, was Beth and Carl; eyes wide with amazement and excitement. As Charlie hastily put the gun away, Beth said, "My uncle Jim can do that."

Still a bit embarrassed, Charlie was slow in understanding what she was saying, "Hi, Kids," he said, playing for time, "you mean that he can draw his gun out and show you, Beth?"

"No, silly; he can make his gun laugh and dance, just like you done."

"So! You've seen this kind of gun show before, have you," Charlie said, squatting back down in the corner and leaning back against the wall, Indian style. He motioned for the kids to join him and they sat in a little circle as they talked.

"Sure. Uncle Jim can do all that stuff; we saw him get up early and wiggle and draw and shoot and load and stuff. He talked a lot about guns and shooting and stuff." She talked as she sat down and gathered her skirt around her knees; smoothing out the wrinkles with her palm. Carl nodded his head in agreement his eyes wide with excitement.

They talked the rest of the afternoon; the kids telling stories about their Dad, Mom and Uncle Jim. The stories were about fort life, Indians, soldiers and incidents that had happened to them in the past. In between the children's stories, Charlie told them about the Indians and how he and Ray had traveled through their camp in the rain and how God had protected them. He continued to tell them of the chase and meeting their father with the soldiers. He also thought that Great Bear and his people were safe enough to tell them of helping the Indians gather their horses in the night and the river meeting and how the Indians were now his friends; emphasizing that God had helped them because he loved all men and wanted them to be friends. The kids hung on his every word; Charlie proved to be an exciting story teller and Charlie came to have an admiration for the McKinley family and the way they lived and raised their children.

They missed supper; the rain deadening the sounds outside, but they didn't mind because Charlie dug out some of his antelope jerky and they ate it like candy while they talked; washing it down from his canteen.

They were so engrossed in their talk that it was starting to get dark before Charlie noticed how late it was. He sighed, "In trouble again," he thought as he pictured how angry Ruth would be. He didn't have to imagine very long, as they started for the door it flew open and in stormed a very worried Ruth, with the Colonel and a handful of the soldiers following, heading for the horses to start a search.

Spying the children, she ran to them, scooped them up in her arms and kissed each one; then she realized what had happened and clouds of anger darkened her face as she looked at Charlie, "Explain!" She made it a one word sentence; a sign Charlie had found meant that a woman was just holding herself in by pure inner strength and he had better have a darn good explanation.

"I'm sorry, Ruth; it's all my fault. They found me putting my packs in order and, seeing as its raining, we stayed in here telling stories and chewing antelope jerky. I lost track of the time until I noticed it getting dark and I knew you would be worried. We were just on our way out, so I could take them home." There was complete silence as she searched his face and saw that that was the truth. One of the soldiers coughed and another shuffled his feet nervously.

Beth stared up at her mother and said, "That's right, Mommy. He's a good story teller and he's friends with the Indians and God, too."

With an effort, that drew more admiration from Charlie, she sighed and, shook off the anger, "I hope you have learned a lesson, Charlie; and you two, too. I was so worried about you. Come on, home with you now."

Over her shoulder she said, "Ray is awake and looking for you, Charlie; I'm still mad tonight, so, I'll see you in the morning."

Charlie's honesty and sincerity had won him a real friend in Ruth and Charlie knew it. As he watched her leave, his eyes made contact with the angry scowl of Colonel Belmont's and he read true the meaning; the Colonel was jealous. He thought he was going to help Ruth and be a hero, in her eyes, and Charlie had taken his opportunity away. The Colonel held his gaze a while longer, then turned with his men, and left Charlie alone with his troubling thoughts.

"Could this situation get any more complicated," Charlie mused as he sat in the dark chewing on a piece of alfalfa. He didn't know that the next few days would answer that question but not to his liking. He shrugged and got up to check on Ray, he had come up with no more answers than he had the day before but he felt that things were getting worse.

Chapter 9

Ray had been glad to see him and they had talked way into the night. She had asked to hear the story of the snake and the boy again after he told it the first time and was curious about the fort and the people in the town. She also told him more about her people and their customs, her parents and about her fear for the marriage that she was arranged into.

Charlie had thought that he heard her hint that, if she chose another man, herself, then she would not have to go back and would not be obligated to go through with their planed marriage; but he pretended that he missed the hint and changed the subject to how tired she must be and that she should rest.

She was still watching him as he gently closed the door on his way out. The bunkhouse full of soldiers was alive with the sounds of men sleeping as Charlie made his way, quietly, to his bunk and turned in. His mind was going over how pretty Ray was and her growing affection for him and he could not sleep immediately. After some struggling with his thoughts and some prayer, he was able to fall asleep, in spite of the noise.

The next morning, after breakfast and a check over from the Major, Ray was shown the chair that she could use. Someone had taken the time to weave wet alder branches together into a very comfortable looking armchair and had made two alder branch wheels, that were built like the wheels on a wagon, fastened to the back legs. The chair sat on its own four legs when it was stood upright but, when it was tipped back, the wheels lifted it off the ground, like a wheelbarrow and it could be pushed around, riding on those wheels. This was the major event of the morning and almost everyone was there.

As Charlie lifted Ray into the chair and made her comfortable, she found a number of opportunities to look him in the eyes and to touch his hand a little more often than necessary. She had taken the time before anyone was around to comb her hair out and now it hung down her back and around both sides of her face, covering a good portion of her shirt front. She had taken her wide beaded belt off and tied it around her forehead and letting the extra length mix with her hair and hang down her back with it.

Charlie had to admit that she radiated beauty as she sat humbly in her chair and looked around at all the men.

The kids wanted desperately to push it, so Charlie offered to help them and, with a child on each side, Charlie wheeled Ray outside on the porch where the sun, having been up for a couple of hours, was warming up the boards making a very comfortable place to rest.

Even though Ray was an Indian, she began winning the hearts of the men with her quick smile and soft voice. She had a way of looking at you as if you were the only person in the world, when you talked to her and, even though she could not understand most of what was said, she made everyone feel special.

Charlie, watching from behind her, also saw the looks of those men who, taking in her beauty, had other thoughts in mind. The one that worried him the most was the intense stare of the Colonel. The saying 'like father, like son' came to Charlie's mind and he knew his trouble had just doubled.

He wheeled Ray over to the bench that was part of the porch furniture and set the chair down beside it. Ruth sat beside Ray on the bench and gave Charlie a knowing look; she had seen the Colonel looking, too.

The men started to drift away to their duties and Charlie sat down beside Ruth as the children began their game of teaching English to Ray; Ruth spoke in a low voice, "first, Charlie, I'm not mad at you anymore. The children told me about your stories and the lessons that you were teaching them about God helping you so much. Thank you! They need another man, besides their father, to show them that God is real; someone they like and trust. I also saw the look the Colonel gave Ray and, I want you to know that, I will help you as much as I can. Todd doesn't know, and I don't want him to find out, but the Colonel tried and would still like to make an impression on me. I'm not so naive as to think he was interested in my personality. He has kept his distance because he is afraid of Todd. In his younger days, Todd enjoyed a little rough play every now and again and would beat two men, like the Colonel, just to have a little fun and he is well liked by all his men."

She continued, when Charlie didn't say anything, "Ray would be a different situation than me. I'm not prejudice when I say that, being an Indian, she would be considered a toy that could be thrown away and no one would care. They will look for a way to get you out of the way so they can have her."

As Ruth talked, the children's and Ray's laughter could be heard as they played. Charlie's mind refused to imagine what sound would be heard if the Belmont's got their way. The same anger that drove him to track the three murderers now started to build in him again. Men; selfishly taking what they wanted and coldly not caring for anyone else made Charlie want to lash out and…the thought went unfinished and, as Charlie took a deep breath, he unclenched his fists that he had unconsciously doubled up.

"I need some suggestions, Ruth; if I leave, they'll send Todd and his soldiers after me and I don't want to run from Todd, and, if I stay, it's their fort and they're in control here." His mind went to the town and what he might find there.

As if she read his mind, Ruth said, "there is a church in town and Reverend Mathew is a good man. His congregation is not real big and he looks for ways to make some extra money to keep going. He may consider taking in some boarders and his wife is a good cook. He has four children, so there would always be someone around most of the time."

The suggestion sounded right and Charlie decided to check into it. Rising, he said, "That sound great. If you'll watch Ray, I think I'll ride into town."

"Of course," she said and Charlie told Ray where he was going, using a few English words that he had heard the kids teaching Ray. Her smile radiated from her, pleased that he was paying attention and that she understood what he said. "Yah," she used the kids' favorite word for yes as she caressed his hand.

Ruth saw the caress and saw the troubled frown that flitted across Charlie's face before he smiled and left. "So much like my Toddy," she thought and, "Lord help him, please."

Charlie saddled Joe and went into town, going to the store first. He bought some candy for the kids and then picked out a man's shirt and pants for Ray, hoping to hide her feminine curves a little. He added a belt with a knife and sheath and found some local Indian made hunting moccasins to replace the ones she had worn ragged while she ran from the Sioux.

Placing his purchases in a gunny sack and tying it to Joe's saddle horn, he took Joe's reins and, more like an Indian than a cowboy, he walked down the street towards the church.

He had to pass the stable on his way and, dropping Joe's reins beside the hitching post, went inside. He had brought another of the extra rifles with him, this morning, thinking to see if Tim would let him give it to Sam. He found the big man oiling the leather on one of the saddles that Charlie had traded to him; cleaning them up so they could be sold.

"Morning, Tim," Charlie said and looking around asked, "is Sam here?"

"Mornin'; he's out back playing."

"Good, I have something that I would like to ask you. I have a couple of spare rifles and I would like to give this one to Sam if you and your wife think that that is alright."

"We don't have one and we could use the extra meat from hunting," Tim was thinking out loud, "but Susan doesn't like guns. I don't think she would let Sam have it; he is only eight."

"Maybe, I could give the rifle to you and between the two of us we could show Sam how to handle it right." Charlie suggested.

Tim's face light up and he said, "It's been a long time since I had a rifle and I used to be a fair shot with one, too."

"Its settled then," and he passed the rifle and bullets to Tim. "I have to go and see the Preacher about a little business so, I'll see you later."

"Thanks," Tim said, not taking his eyes off of the gun, "Pastor Dan is a right nice man and he'll be glad to see you."

"Your welcome, Tim; see you later." He said as he left the stable and continued on to the church. It was a rough-hewn board 4x4 building with one huge room and a door in each wall. [4x4 meant that it was as long as it was wide] There were two windows per wall, one on each side of the doors and it was full of a variety of chairs and benches all facing a little raised platform with a book podium in one corner of the room.

After passing through the church and finding no-one, he found Reverend Dan Mathew out back weeding a rather large garden. Reverend Mathew, seeing him coming, leaned his hoe against a fence, running around the garden, and came to meet him, extending his hand. "Welcome, friend," he said with a genuine sincerity.

He was a big man that Charlie liked immediately. His hands were calloused from work and his arms and shoulders bulged with much used muscles; although his wide midsection spoke of eating well. His handshake was firm and matched Charlie's for grip. His face was wide, with wide set eyes and a big nose and mouth; his loose wavy brown hair fell down halfway to his shoulders and was only kept back from his eyes by his constantly running his fingers through it.

"Reverend Mathew?" Charlie asked. "Please, call me Dan," was his reply, a question in his eyes.

"Charlie; I'm pleased to meet you."

"Well, Charlie; most people do not come to church on Thursday, so, how can I help you?" Charlie liked his 'direct to the point' approach. Dan led the way to a bench and small table set up under a young fruit tree in the center of the garden. Before they could sit down, a young girl came running down a well worn path from a house beside the church, with a picture of liquid and a couple of mugs. The garden was so large that it backed onto several of the houses on this side of the street but the church and this house seemed to be about the center.

When the girl arrived, Dan introduced her as his daughter, Sally; she gave a small courtesy and a shy smile. She was a pretty girl of about ten with blonde hair and big blue eyes. When she saw that the men did not want anything else, she turned and ran back to the house.

Charlie was surprised to find the liquid was lemon juice and his questioning look brought the explanation from Dan; a wagon train with some of his friends had just passed through from California with what remained of a load of lemons and Dan had bought the last of them to make lemonade and put it in his root cellar to stay cold. He was selling it locally to get some extra money to live on.

As they sat down, Charlie came right to the point also, explaining that he had a hurt Indian girl and needed a place to stay while he waited for Arthur and the soldiers to return to release him from their suspicions. He told Dan most of the situation with Ray, minimizing the obsession part but voicing his concern about white men in general; giving him the idea but not the danger involved. Charlie considered that his part to handle.

Dan listened patiently and, when Charlie was done, asked, "So, how did you come to me and what can I do?" And again, Charlie was honest and told him what Ruth had said about renting a room from him and that Tim said that he was a good man.

Dan looked at him for a while, taking in the clothes and the way he wore his guns, then surprising Charlie again, he said, "Tim is an honest, simple soul and I heard what you did for Him and Sam. My thanks, also; Tim is the deacon of our church. He, Susan and Sam are well thought of by my family and me. Now, what is this girl to you and what trouble are you in?"

Charlie leveled with him and told him about the Belmont's desire for Ray and that aside from her possessiveness, he was only looking out for her.

Dan gave him a serious look and said, "I like an honest man. Lets ask Momma what she thinks God would have us do in this situation." And he led the way to the house.

It was not a big house but it was as neat and as clean as any Charlie had seen out west. Working at the table was a small woman with a calm face and work-worn hands. Her blond hair was pulled back and tied in a bun behind her head but a few strands had worked their way loose and were continually having to be brushed back from her face. Charlie noticed the similar work habits and character habits between husband and wife and realized that they were a very close family. She had two daughters working with her in the kitchen, the room facing the garden; she introduced the other daughter as Rachel and, even though she was much younger than her sister, she was working right along side of her with a serious look about her. She was thinner than her sister and had a touch of red in her blond hair but the facial similarities were evident.

Dan started right in with, "Ann, this young man has a problem," and he told her what Charlie and he had been talking about.

The women listened while they worked and, when Dan was done, they had dinner ready and were setting the table. Before anyone could give their opinion, Ann said, "You and Charlie clean up, dinner is ready. Decisions can be made after you eat." It was not a request for him to stay but a statement of fact that he was.

Dan agreed and led the way outside to the wash basin where they were joined by two boys, home for dinner from their jobs in town. Dan introduced Matthew, the oldest and John, a couple of years younger. Charlie recognized Matthew as the clerk from the general store.

When they were seated for dinner, they waited for Dan and, when he saw that they were all here, he bowed his head and said grace; Charlie gladly following their lead and echoing their "Amen".

They ate in relative silence and Charlie could feel the covert glances that he was getting from everyone, although he was not uncomfortable because they made him feel welcome and accepted. When they were done, Ann shooed them into another room and told the girls to clean up the table. The boys went back to their jobs and, when Dan, Ann and Charlie were seated, Ann said, "We can bunk the girl with ours and you can sleep in the stable, Charlie," Dan nodded while she talked, "You'll pay a dollar fifty a day board, meals included. Where the girl is hurt, she can rest and recover; you can help some in the garden." Even though she said it as if it was already agreed, she raised a questioning eyebrow at Charlie.

Charlie thought for a minute, then said, "Two fifty a day; I will help in the garden, when I can and you allow Beth and Carl to visit Ray, whenever they are allowed, to teach her English and allow Rachel to help them?"

Dan laughed, "You know you're throwing your money away. If she could, Rachel would pay you to have a couple of kids to play with and an Indian girl to teach English to. I think it's a deal, don't you mamma?" Ann nodded her head, smiling. Charlie had made another good impression and felt good about this family's friendship.

He had stayed most of the afternoon helping Dan in his garden and listening to half a dozen sermons from the big man; he couldn't complain, he had preach one or two himself and they had parted good friends. He made it back to the fort in time to eat supper with Ray, Ruth and the kids. Over the meal, he told them of the deal he had made with the Mathew and promised Ruth that he would take and return the kids personally when she let them go to see Ray.

"You might not have to," she said, "their Uncle Jim will be here tomorrow for a visit and he would be staying at the hotel."

"That's great news." Charlie said enthusiastically, "I'm looking forward to meeting this Jim McKinley." Ruth laughed, "Not McKinley; he's my brother, Jim Marshall."

Jim Marshall; even though Charlie was still laughing and talked on with them, it felt like he had been hit in the stomach with a big club. No wonder the kids had said that he could make his guns laugh and dance; Jim Marshall was reported to be one of the deadliest gunslingers west of the Mississippi River.

Most of the fast gunmen that you will hear about in the east have had some newspaper reporter write about them; sparking people's imaginations and building reputations. Then there are those that are only known in the west; fast, deadly, quiet men that don't speak about what they have done and are only known by the most serious listeners and old-timers that have lived long and seen much. Jim Marshall was one of these men; quiet, confident and only known by a few men. Charlie had listened to the oldsters' tales and remembered them now.

They say that Jim always produces when he is hired to do a job and, it didn't matter how fast they were, all the men that Jim had killed had their guns drawn and were shot in the front. Jim also never drew first but always let the other man start his draw and then killed him. Two or three of the names that Charlie had heard that Jim had bested with his guns, he had heard from other sources that they were indeed fast men with their guns but obviously not fast enough when they drew against Jim.

The fact that he was Ruth's brother and Todd's brother-in-law made it worse; Todd was Army, and the Army, meaning the Belmont's, might send Todd after Charlie. Anything could happen in a situation like that and, if it was a disaster, Charlie could lose his reputation, the friendships that he had made here and, even, his life.

Charlie prayed inwardly, "Lord, what are you doing to me?" Feeling the need to seek some older mans advice, he asked where Major Stewart was and was told that someone from Arthur's patrol came and took him out to the patrol. They said that he was urgently needed there.

Charlie went to bed that night with a lot of unanswered questions; the answers were coming but not to Charlie's liking.

The next morning promised to be a beautiful clear sunny day and, again, Charlie ate with Ray, Ruth and the kids. He found their company better than being stared at by the Colonel and the food was better. They made the decision together to move Ray into town; Ruth and the kids would come along and wait for Uncle Jim and Charlie, after checking Ray's wound, thought that she would have no trouble riding in the travois.

The decision made, Charlie went to the stable to load his packs and get the horses ready. He had put the packages that he had bought in the stable and, when he returned, brought them with him. Everyone was ready to go; Ruth had packed a lunch so they could make it a picnic.

"I've got something for you," he said to Ray; still using sign language but putting in some English that he knew she understood. While they watched he brought out the shirt, pants, moccasins and knife belt. The knife and moccasins were expected Indian gifts and Ray smiled prettily and held them up for all to see but she frowned at the shirt and pants. Charlie turned to Ruth for help, "To help cover her up; you know her girl looks," he fumbled.

Understanding, Ruth gave him a sharp look that only said one word; 'men!', then took the shirt and held it up. It would fit well and was fashionable for the area; she turned it around and, after a moment, smiled and nodded to Ray. Being reassured, Ray beamed her gratitude with a huge smile. She would like to wear them to town and needed help getting them on so Charlie took the kids and went to get the horses.

When they returned Ray and Ruth were outside on the porch. The new clothes did little to hide Ray's beauty even if they reduced the exposure of her feminine curves and Charlie saw Colonel Belmont watching them from the porch of his office. He gently picked her up and put her on the travois; just for safe measures he was using Joe again for it. He had Nails, Ruth had an Army horse, Molly carried the two kids; the little paint horse was packed heavily with all their belongings. It was not far to town and she seemed to enjoy doing what was asked of her.

Charlie put the chair with wheels on Joe's back and they started out.

The kids ate candy, teased each other and made the trip to town into an adventure into the wilderness; by the time they reached town they were all sore from laughing and shouting. It was like a circus coming to town; the people stopped and stared as they entered. Charlie knew that the gossip tongues would be wagging and, even though he did not want it, he knew that everyone for miles around would know what was taking place, in just a few days.

The Mathew met them at their door and showed them to the bedroom Ray would be sharing with Sally and Rachel. Matthew and John were away to their jobs, uptown but the girls were home and had seen Beth and Carl when they were in town before but had not gotten the chance to meet them, so, after the introductions, the four kids gathered around Ray and talked and signed, getting to know each other. While Ruth and Ann talked, Dan followed Charlie to the stable where he helped him care for his horses. "If you want, you can run them in the corral with ours," he said and Charlie saw two large harness horses watching them from inside a rail fenced enclosure.

Charlie's feelings were boiling inside him but he did not dare let them show. He had no one that knew him enough and that he knew to trust with his worry. He had been crying out to God but God seemed to be sitting on the side not answering him. He was just about to confide in Dan when Dan said, "You make yourself to home; I think I'll go work in the garden some," and he turned and strode out the back door.

Charlie frowned and leaned on the stable door post, looking out towards the house where he could see the kids. He included Ray in that phrase because she was so young and she related to the others so easily. Charlie had lived a life of independence; after leaving home, had looked after himself. He had grown muscle hard from hardships, fast with his guns and fists by necessity, wise and careful on the trail to survive but he had had only himself and he could come and go as he pleased. Alone, he probably would have ignored Arthur's threat and rode away. Joe was fast and tough and it would have taken a very good horse just to stay with him. Charlie had learned from some of the best teachers when it came to losing a tracker on his trail; he had no doubt that he could have gotten away and this whole situation avoided.

Now he had the responsibility to look after Ray and the trouble that wanted to swallow her up and, he found that that burden was a heavy one to carry. The odds against him seemed to be getting bigger and bigger everyday and he didn't know how to stop or change them.

His one comfort was that he knew God was watching and he knew God was in control; he would just have to go on faith and trust Him no matter how hard it would get.

On an impulse, he took the three dead brother's saddlebags and dumped the contents into a pile on one of the horse blankets. He carefully sorted through it; taking out papers, jewelry and other personal things that could connect him to those men.

Then he carefully searched the guns, holsters and saddle for any identification marks; he found none. Repacking the saddlebags with food and other ordinary things, he took the personal items and put them in a burlap sack. Shouldering the sack and taking his new Henry rifle, he saddled Joe and went to the house.

"If you don't need me, I have this new rifle that I would like to true-up. I thought that I could go down by the river and shoot it in." He communicated in sign and English to include everybody. They were caught up in the excitement of their visit and all bid him to have fun and went back to their talks and games. Ray's eyes lingered on him longer than necessary and had a proud and possessive gleam in them.

He swung by the store to buy more bullets and, as he paid for them, Matthew confided in him; "The people that I talk to are speculating that you are some great outlaw or gunslinger wanted for murder somewhere and here to hide out. They're saying that no normal person could have killed that snake and been so accurate."

He continued, not waiting for Charlie to say anything, "Most people around here are quick to think the worst of others but," and his eyes brightened, "That was some shot. There were two small grooves in the top of the rock less than an inch apart where the bullets had touched it as they went over it."

Hiding his surprise, Charlie thanked Matthew, telling him that he would see him later. His brain worked on his worry as he left town on Joe; he had not known that evidence of his accuracy had been left in the rock or that he was becoming so famous so fast. People's imaginations could create more trouble if he were not more careful.

CHAPTER 10

Down by the water, he found a bank that he could use as a bullet backstop. First he read all the papers looking for information as to what they were. A number of papers held his attention for some time and he carefully folded them and put them in a hidden pocket in his holster belt.

His holster was custom built so that the guns overlapped just above his crotch. The butts of the guns stuck out each side within easy reach of his hands and the guns were sloped downwards at the barrels so the holster could be made of one piece of leather going across his stomach. It was high enough to sit on his lap when he sat down or rode in his saddle and placed the gun butts right where his hands and wrists met when he was ready to draw. His hands only had to travel a few inches to close on the gun butts and another few inches to clear the holsters already being almost pointed when they were clear of their holster. Built into the back of the holster was a solid hidden pocket where he kept ten double eagle coins, for a back-up, and any important papers that he had. The belt buckle sat over the gun barrels with the handles protruding out beside it, one on each side.

The jewelry and personal items, he was sure, were stolen and he put them under a rock behind a large pine tree growing at the bottom of the river bank; between two root outcrops.

The rest of the papers he set up side by side against the bank, being held with a little dirt at their corners. Walking away fifty paces, he found a down tree to rest the rifle on and started shooting at the first piece of paper; aiming for its center. After three shots he went to the paper to see how far he was shooting from where he had aimed, then he would correct the front sight and shoot a few more times. He continued shooting and adjusting until he was satisfied the gun was true and the papers were destroyed.

Next, he took his knife and scored the pine's bark; making a mark about the size of a silver dollar. He turned and walked away; at thirty paces he spun, drew both guns and fired; continuing until both guns were empty. Anyone watching would not have seen the draw and only heard one continuous roar as the guns bucked in his hands. It was over in seconds. As he walked back to the pine tree a drop of sweat ran down to the end of his nose and he wiped it away; surprised that he had been concentrating that hard.

The score in the bark was gone and there was torn tree bark instead. Charlie put his hand over the torn bark and, when he did, he covered the hole. All twelve shots had hit an area less than six inches across. Charlie knew that that was good fast shooting but, if it came to shooting between him and Jim, was that good enough? Charlie hoped he would never have to find out.

Shrugging, he cut two more holes in the bark; one a foot above the first and one a foot below the first; then he went back to the spot he had stood in the handgun flourish.

Facing away from the tree, he spun to the right, drawing his right hand gun and firing before he stopped. Then he did the same with the left hand gun; spinning to the left. This was the hardest maneuver for accuracy that Charlie knew; the spin, the draw and the shot all going in the same direction often made the gun shoot past the target. He practiced this move some more and then changed his positions for firing; lying down, on one knee, twisting backwards and rolling to a stop to fire.

The gun seemed to have a life of its own and, every time Charlie shot at the tree, bark and chips flew.

After an hour, Charlie was satisfied that he was as good as his practice could make him and he cleaned and reloaded all his guns; giving them a light oiling before putting them away. On impulse, he took out his knife and made a pass or two at an imaginary foe; then, dropping into a knife fighter's stance he went through another half hour of cuts and jabs. His technique was his own; he had learned that a good knife man keyed his moves to what he did naturally. By doing this, it felt right and could be done faster and with more confidence. Charlie looked more like a dancer than a killer; he moved with ease and speed instead of erratic force.

A good knife fighter did not try to stab or hack his opponents but, using the last three inches of blade, cut whatever he could of his opponent without getting cut in return. A three inch deep cut on an arm or wrist could really hinder his opponent into making some major mistakes and, if a tendon or artery were cut, might end the fight without a death.

When Charlie was satisfied with his speed and timing, he spent another half hour playing with his knife, juggling and spinning it; keeping familiar with its weight and feel.

All this time, Joe had been eating grass upriver a few hundred yards; his saddle and bridle lying in a pile next to the bank. As Charlie put the knife away and looked at Joe, Joe raised his head and looked up the bank and slightly further upriver. A man's hat appeared followed by his head, shoulders and a horse, as he rode to the top of the bank and over it, coming down to where Charlie stood watching.

He rode easy and relaxed in the saddle but his hand was too near his gun to be there by chance. He was a well built man, broad across the shoulders and tapering down to a narrow waist. His clothes were plain cowboy dress and his boots were well worn. The plainness ended there, his horse was a big black gelding, all chest and legs; built for speed and endurance. His gun rig also stood out, a tooled leather holster and belt with a black handled six-gun sitting in a cross-draw holster. He was right handed but he carried his gun on his left hip, butt turned in towards his right hand.

Charlie couldn't see his facial features because his hat was pulled down shading his eyes and upper face. He only made out a light colored and neatly trimmed beard.

As he slowly rode towards him, Charlie saw his head turn slightly one way and then the other and he knew that the man was looking at what Charlie had done.

Neither of them spoke and, when the stranger had ridden to within ten feet of Charlie, he stopped. Charlie now saw his light brown hair, straight nose and blue eyes; eyes that were studying him casually. Charlie waited, doing some studying of his own and having a vague feeling of familiarity. This stranger's features were so much like his own that he could almost be called a family member but Charlie had not seen this man before today.

He was about Charlie's age and had traveled some distance; he was covered with road dust, his clothes were wrinkled and he looked tired in spite of his active eyes. There was a confident air about him; a feeling of strength and knowledge. He didn't look like the ordinary run-of-the-mill gunslinger but he did look like a man to be reckoned with when trouble came his way.

Charlie decided to speak first and extent a friendly invitation, "light and sit, stranger" and he sat on the downed tree he had been standing beside.

"Thank you, Charlie. Don't mind if I do," and he dismounted, giving Charlie time to get over his surprise at him knowing his name.

"You have the advantage on me; do I know you?"

"No, Charlie, we've never met but I've kept my ears open to your comings and goings for some time now. You can call me Dick." Walking over and sitting on the other end of the tree, he casually waved a hand at the pine, "Planning on starting a war?"

The way he said it told Charlie that he was just making conversation, not digging for information.

"Just practicing; I try not to start any wars but you never know when one might drop in uninvited like."

"That's true," Dick replied, "it pays to be ready."

As they continued to talk, it became obvious to Charlie that Dick knew quite a lot about him but was not telling Charlie very much about himself. Finally, Dick mentioned, "I'm heading into town, mind if I ride along with you?"

With all of Charlie's problem's, he was glad to have someone around that was friendly without wanting or needing anything, "Sure, I'll get my horse." Whistling for Joe, he headed for his saddle. Joe met him there and, after saddling up, they headed for town.

They kept the conversation open and friendly as they made their way back to town. Charlie found out that Dick's horse was named 'Stop-it' and the stories that Dick told about the many times that he caught his big black horse doing things that he wasn't supposed to earned him that name kept them both amused.

Like Charlie and Joe, Dick and Stop-it had developed a personal relationship with each other and Stop-it loved to take Dick's things and move them; like his blanket or his boot and he had a love of taking Dick's hat off and dropping it on the ground.

As they rode up the street to the Mathew' house, Charlie found that it was easy talking to Dick and he seemed to have accepted Charlie as his friend.

They had missed the noon meal and, seeing no-one around outside the Mathews's house, Charlie invited Dick to eat at the hotel eating house; which he accepted.

They left their horses at the rack and went in. The restaurant was empty but they could see the remains of crumbs on empty tables where their patrons had eaten their noon-day meals and could hear the racket from the kitchen as the help cleaned the dishes. There were a number of bare wooden tables scattered around the room, each with a pair or more of rickety looking wooden chairs; nothing fancy but the smell of cooked food was still inviting. They found a table near the back, by the kitchen doorway, in the corner. Both placed the wall at their backs, facing the room. From their vantage point, they could look through the windows into the street and also see through the doorway into the attached hotel lobby.

The waitress entered from the back room and was a slip of a girl in her late teens; she was plain looking with a weak chin and sharp facial features. Her shoulder-length brown hair was neglected and her clothes were wrinkled. She seemed to have a permanent frown on her face and, when she talked, it was in monotone; as if she was drained of all emotion. "Special today is steak and potatoes. Want some coffee?"

Charlie, raising an eyebrow at Dick and receiving a nod, ordered; "That would be fine for both of us, thanks." She shuffled away heading for the kitchen again, her bare feet making little pat patting noises as she walked.

They both watched her leave, wondering what had happened in her life to take the joy out of her. Charlie turn back to speak to Dick but caught himself as boot steps in the lobby drew their attention. They had not noticed the outside door open, in the other room, but the owner of one of the pair of boots was making no effort to walk quietly.

Watching the doorway, both saw two men walk past it, heading for the desk clerk. The first was a thin man dressed all in black; fancy black shinny boots matched his black holster belt, tied down to each leg with two matching, pearl handled pistols. Swaggering as he walked, the dark complexioned man's mouth was sneering and his dark eyes were mere slits as he approached the clerk.

Charlie started, it was Lin; his friend from the gold camps. While he had been teaching Charlie to use his hands to fight, Charlie had taught him how to use a gun and he had learned surprisingly fast.

What surprised Charlie more was the words he heard Dick say under his breath, "Johnny Gringo!" Johnny Gringo! One of the fastest and deadliest gun-slicks to ever live; they say that he would go out of his way to pick a gunfight just for the fun of it. Charlie clamped his mouth shut; he had to find out more, before he said anything.

The second man was bigger and taller, dressed in a gamblers black suit; he was black haired and sported a wide handlebar mustache and a goatee. His two-gun, tied down holster was tooled leather and the gun butts were black walnut.

Dick was still thinking out loud, "And Jim Marshall; why would he be traveling with Johnny Gringo?" There was no fear in his voice, only thoughtful contemplation.

Their food arrived, everything brought on a tray by the sad-faced waitress and dispersed in front of them with practiced efficiency; halting further conversation and, without hesitation, Charlie bowed his head and said grace. When he was done, he was pleased to hear a hearty "Amen" from Dick. This told him much about his new friend.

As they ate, they both unconsciously followed the action in the hotel lobby. Johnny and Jim signed in and had their bags sent to their room, then they came into the restaurant.

Charlie ducked his head and pretended to be heartily eating but he heard Johnny's foot-steps as he came to their table. "You looking for me, Dick?" he said.

"Not yet, Johnny; why are you expecting me to?" was his reply.

Charlie glanced at Dick and saw that he was pale but he was trying not to show it.

"I'll be in town for a few days, if you want to find me you won't have to look far," and he laughed, obviously enjoying the challenge that he was taunting Dick with.

Charlie could stand it no longer; this wasn't the Lin he had known. This man was making him mad. He looked up and into the black eyes of a very surprised Johnny Gringo. His laughter ended and the silence held for a few brief seconds while the waitress stood poised in the middle of the room and Jim waited, frowning, with his hand on his chair at a table across the room.

Recognition flashed across Johnny's, AKA Lin's, face and with an effort he pulled himself together. Not taking his eyes away from Charlie, he snarled "I'll see you later, Dick", and then he turned and went back to the table that he shared with Jim.

Dick's hand trembled ever so slightly as he lifted his coffee cup for a drink but it was gone when he set the cup back down. He turned his head towards Charlie and the smile of thanks was so small that no-one except Charlie saw it.

Charlie's anger was a little slower at leaving; he hated people who pushed others around but he really hated pushy, rude bullies. There was other ways to create fear in people than to be physically strong and Johnny Gringo was using the fact that he was cruel and deadly with his guns to create fear in everyone around him.

When they were done their meal, Johnny and Jim were still eating and having their own private conversation. Charlie paid for the meal and gave the waitress a larger than normal tip; he thought she looked like she could use a lift. He didn't see the long lingering look she gave him as they left or notice that both Johnny and Jim looked up to watch them leave.

They headed for the Mathew' house; Charlie wanted to check on Ray and tell Ruth that her brother was in town.

The children saw them first and ran, squealing to meet them; Charlie picked Carl up and, after tickling him, set him on Dick's shoulders and then picked up Beth and Rachel in each arm and they walked up to the porch and where he deposited the three kids. The three immediately jumped on Charlie and tried to take him down and tickle him. Charlie let himself be upset and they went down in a pile of arms and legs, squealing and laughing; thoroughly enjoying this new game.

When they let him up, Ruth and Ann had pushed Ray, in her chair, out onto the porch and were standing there laughing as well.

Laughing, Charlie said, "Your raising a bad bunch of roughens here, ladies."

Still hardly able to contain her laughter, Ruth replied, "You're the bad influence, you big bully."

While they were settling down on the porch, Dan came around the corner of the house. It didn't take him long to size up the situation and he found a seat to enjoy the banter.

After a time of teasing and fun, Charlie introduced Dick and he was welcomed all round.

Sobering a little, Charlie told Ruth that they had seen her brother at the hotel and the conversation took on a more serious note.

Dan had heard of Johnny Gringo and was not pleased that he was here but, if he was with Ruth's brother, they would do what they could to welcome him.

They showed Charlie where Ray was staying and the kids showed off the words that Ray was learning. She was like a sun beam as she repeated the words and there meanings for Charlie. It was obvious to everyone that she thought the sun rose and set on Charlie; she hardly took her eyes off of him. Whenever he was near her she would touch his hand or lean towards him; making Charlie uncomfortable because, he knew, it was not supposed to be this way. He kept telling himself that she was a kid and she would get over him but he knew that he was fooling himself.

Dick had also proved himself a hit with the kids and Charlie's suggestion that he bunk in the stable with him brought instant support; Dan agreed and another half dollar was added to the daily rent for his meals. They also agreed to share the garden chores and added hunting for fresh meat besides; they were to start in the morning.

Ruth left the children in Charlie's care with the instructions not to spoil them any more on penalty of having to do dishes for a month if he did. Feinting fear, Charlie agreed. She headed up town to locate her brother, Jim.

After Dan went back to his garden, Charlie and Dick took Ray and the kids to the barn to put their horses away and while they were there, Charlie roped the little paint horse and brought her over to Ray.

"Yours," he said and signed.

"Oh, Olla!" she exclaimed "Olla, Olla", and its name became "Olla" which meant "pretty" in her language. Olla, gentle as ever, nudged Ray's hand and accepted her touches.

Showing her the saddle and bridle, he made her understand that they were hers also. She made a face at him but shook her head, yes. The kids loved it and made a big fuss over her.

Dick watched what was happening with his new friend and a new admiration started to grow in him for this Charlie Power.

They spent the afternoon talking and playing; sometimes rubbing down the horses, the next teaching Ray some more English. They ended the afternoon sitting in a circle tossing a sack ball back and forth and telling stories. Charlie's being the most interesting and requested but they loved Dick's story of how Stop-it got his name.

When it was time for supper, they all went to the house where they came upon Ruth standing by the porch talking to her brother. The kids screeched and ran for him and, being caught up in his arms, hugged him. Both tried to talk at once.

Charlie and Dick moved to go by them into the house but Ruth beckoned for them to wait and, when the kids were done, brought Jim over and introduced them to him.

"Jim, this is our good friend Charlie and his friend Dick." And "Charlie, Dick, meet my brother, Jim"

There was a reserved expression on Jim's face but he said "Pleased to meet you, Charlie; Dick." No one shook hands but their eyes were busily evaluating the others size and the way they wore their guns and the ease of their movements.

Charlie ventured, "Seen you at the hotel at noon, Jim, so I told Ruth you were here. She came in this morning to meet you. The kids have been telling me about you; seems they think a lot of you." He left the hint there that Jim might try living up to the kids' expectations of him. It was a bold move for Charlie but, he figured, the kids were worth the gamble.

Jim caught the dig and color started to show around his collar but the kids hugged him and Carl said, "Love Jim."

Beth shushed him and said, 'Your not s'posed to love a man, silly."

Charlie quickly spoke and said, "You're supposed to love family, though, Beth and, I think, it's OK this time." Ruth confirmed, "Yes, he is your uncle and it's OK.

Jim gave Charlie a sharp penetrating look but did not say any more.

The rest of the conversation was strained but, when the time came for them to eat, they were starting to relax.

119

Dan had set up a table outside, picnic fashion, because there were so many of them and, after he said grace, they dug in and ate their fill.

Charlie watched as Matthew and John tried to make conversation with Ray. Being closer to their age, he knew that they were more interested in her as a girl than as a kid to play games with. He relaxed as he saw their actions were respectful of her gender and not like the attentions of the Belmont's. Dan was raising his boys right; they would be respected men in their own times.

A number of times throughout the meal, Charlie caught Jim's eyes on him and he wondered what that might mean until, almost at the end when everyone was relaxing, he found himself beside Jim, as if by accident.

"Johnny knows you." He said; low enough that no one else could hear.

"Yes. I know your friend."

"He's no friend of mine." Jim was quick to say, "We were just traveling in the same direction. We worked together once." And he moved away.

Thoughtfully, Charlie watched him go, "Strange." He commented out loud.

"How so?" Dick was just getting to him.

"Tell you later," he said. He noticed the girls were clearing the dishes and he said to Ruth; "Am I on the hook for dishes for a month?" She laughed and replied, "No, the kids had fun. You and Dick are good sitters." Changing the subject she said, "Jim wants to see us back to the fort; I hope you don't mind."

"Mind, no. He's family. Use Molly as long as you want. As long as we are here, we don't need her."

After they had left, Rachel and Sally took Ray to bed early; she still tired quickly. The five men sat on the porch, talking quietly and getting to know each other. As the sun set, it got quiet, as if they were reflecting. Then Dan spoke, "Trouble is coming, you can feel it." And, after a long pause, he continued; "Someone is going to die." Matthew and John looked at each other and then at Charlie.

Charlie and Dick said nothing; they both felt the same thing.

CHAPTER 11

When Dan went in to go to bed, Charlie took Dick and they went to look the town over. They walked along one side of the street looking at the buildings and noting allies and out buildings. Each made observations and comments and Charlie told him about what Jim had said.

As they passed the stable, Tim and Sam were coming out. Charlie waved and said, "Tim, Sam, I want you to meet a friend of mine; this is Dick."

They greeted each other and Charlie could see that Dick was as impressed as he had been at the size and gentleness of Tim.

They found out that Tim was just getting off work and he insisted that they go home with him so Charlie could meet his wife, Susan. She had to thank him for saving Sam's life and for the gift of the rifle.

The four made their way to the outskirts of town where Tim had built a one-room log house; the only one in town. He had taken great care and time to build it well. The logs were hand adzed planed, to fit very close together so they needed very little chinking between them to keep the winter draft out and the moss chinking had a good coat of dried river mud over it. He had put a foot of sod for the roof and the grass was growing live on top of it. It would be easy to heat in the winter and cool in the summer. He had built a wide veranda on the front with a stone floor. He told them that he piled his fire wood on it in the fall and then took from the inside first. This gave him a winter entry room to face north to break the wind and to use as a pantry for food.

A heavy set motherly looking woman rose from the chair that she was sitting in on the veranda as they approached. Her face was round and always seemed to be smiling and her blue eyes danced with laughter to match. Her brown hair was combed but coming loose and her cheeks were red but the hand she extended to greet Charlie and Dick was work rough and calloused. Her handshake had the strength of any two men and Charlie noticed Dick wince as she vigorously shook his hand.

Her voice always had the sound like she was happy, even while she seriously thanked Charlie for saving Sam she sounded like she would break out laughing at any minute but Charlie knew that she was thanking him from the bottom of her heart when he saw the tear that crept down from her eye.

Susan was a natural host, keeping the conversation going and drawing their stories from them as she prepared coffee and sweets. Tim sat contentedly by in his armchair; quietly letting her talk and Sam found a place beside Charlie, listening to his every word. Charlie could tell that he wanted to ask him questions but his parents had taught him well and he respected their right to talk first.

Two hours later, Charlie and Dick got up to leave. The time had gone by so fast as they enjoyed each other so much. Charlie was again a success at story telling and was glad to find such friends as these here.

The parting banter was punctuated with laughter as they left Tim's home.

Coming back through town they were passing the saloon when Charlie glanced in through the window. What he saw made him suddenly stop and, peering closer, he saw Lin, Johnny Gringo, sitting and drinking with Colonel Belmont. A cold shiver ran down his spin and he turned to Dick, "its best if we don't let them see us."

As they continued on, Charlie told Dick what he had seen and added, "I wonder what they are cooking up? You knew Johnny from somewhere?" He was breaking a western tradition by asking that but he was hoping to learn more and trusted in their friendship to carry it through.

Dick did not take offence and said; "Yes, it was a small place called Soldier Summit in Utah during a cattle war. The SS ranch was owned by a well liked man named Sam Summit. They called him Soldier Sam because he was a Union veteran. The town was young and he had helped fight off the Indians, the Confederates and the Carpetbaggers to keep the town safe and peaceful."

[Carpetbaggers were rich Union supporters that were land and money hungry.]

"The 88 moved in from down south somewhere; some people said they were from Texas; I don't really know, but Johnny came with them. The 88 herds kept getting bigger and the SS herds kept getting smaller; then the shooting started. They both hired gunslingers but none of them were as fast as Johnny. I heard that he called one youngster down so bad that he had to draw or be branded a yellow coward and then he killed him. Kid had just a cowhand and was only fifteen.

They ended up killing old Sam in a "fair fight"; at least that's what they called it and nobody was there to say any different.

They say that Johnny is not really a white man and that he uses the name "Johnny Gringo" to insult us. Some say he's a Mexican or something."

Charlie listened quietly and, when Dick was done, said, "Yeh, I knew him when he was 'or something'. I wonder what happened to him; he was a friend of mine then."

Dick waited but Charlie decided not to go into more detail just yet.

By this time they were back at the stable and, being talked out decided to turn in. Tomorrow would be another day and would have its own troubles for Charlie.

The east was just starting to turn grey on another clear day when Charlie and Dick came out of the stable with their saddled horses. They set about preparing the wood and doing the morning chores for breakfast.

Dan came out on the porch as they were finishing up and sat down to read his bible; Charlie and Dick joined him and, while they waited for Ann and the girls to cook breakfast had a bible discussion. Hearing the excited talking, Matthew and John joined in to listen.

They were still in a lively discussion when they were called for breakfast and continued the talk at the table; much to Ann's frustration and the girls' interest. Ann had to dodge waving hands and gestures to put the food in front of the men. By this time Dan's face was a getting a nice shade of red and his eyes were going from side to side trying to look at everyone at the same time.

Charlie watched as Dick was trying to answer him word for word; amusement playing around the corners of his mouth.

They had wheeled Ray to the end of the table and she watched in fascination as the three talked; enjoying each wave of their hands and excited comments. Even though she could not understand, she was happy to see Charlie enjoying it so much.

Grace was a little hurried because they were so engrossed but they hoped that the Lord wouldn't mind. The topic was on salvation and how important it was and how important it was to accept Jesus as their savior early and not wait.

They continued until Charlie and Dick were on their horses and ready to leave to go hunting. There Dan, with a huge grin on his face, said; "Boys, you just gave me Sunday morning's sermon. God be with you today and I'll see you later." With that he turned and headed for the church.

Ray, now sitting on the porch, waved as they turned to look back, as they turned past the corner of the stable. Charlie had checked her wound before bedtime, last night, and he thought that she might be able to walk about some today.

He had paid the Mathew a couple of weeks in advance and had left another twenty dollars, in their care, in case Ray needed anything.

It was one of those totally peaceful mornings; the sun shone on the quiet fields where the birds were singing and the insects buzzed. They let the horses pick their own pace which was a brisk walk and the dust hung in the air behind them like a flag. The day was too nice to be disturbed by more talk and they conversed in single word sentences while they watched the day grow around them.

They hadn't gone very far when another rider left town; they recognized Colonel Belmont's uniform, even though they were a quarter of a mile away and heading in a different direction. It was obvious that he had spent the night somewhere in town and was heading back to the fort. Charlie and Dick speculated on this. After seeing him talking to Johnny Gringo, where he had spent last night would have been useful information, they concluded.

"Might not hurt to hang around town, tonight, and ask a question or two" Charlie commented casually before they lost sight of the Colonel as he reached the fort.

"Might not hurt at all" Dick added, also wanting to find out what Johnny and Jim were up to.

They headed northwest, out into the plain; almost the same path that Charlie and Ray had taken coming here. They had brought Nails with them hoping to get a buffalo and pack the meat back on him. He welcomed the chance to be out again and, as they had no lead rope on him, he willingly trotted alongside Joe; his nose almost touching Charlie's knee.

Charlie believed in gentle breaking his animals. He found that they were more willing to be around him and do the things he wanted them to do than if he was rough on them.

As the morning progressed they started moving faster, wanting to make a swing north and east. If they found buffalo, they would be able to see them for a long way off so they did not have to hide and sneak up on their game. They kept their eyes roving over the countryside, though, because you never know when a deer, elk or antelope might be near.

Charlie had his Sharps rifle and had loaned his Henry to Dick; it had a little more range than his single-shot carbine.

They were continuing their idol conversations and getting to know each other better and, by ten o'clock were riding parallel to a wash with a small stream running in it. They were riding just below the edge so they could look over the top without being seen when Charlie spotted the herd of elk grazing beside the tree-line at the edge of the stream that they had come to and were following north. They were a little ways ahead of them and did not hear Charlie and Dick coming.

Charlie motioned to Dick, who finally saw them, and he nodded. They dropped down lower off the sky-line and, when they were opposite the elk, dismounted. Taking their rifles, they secured the horses and eased to the top of the hill. They knelt down, at the top, and crawled until they could look down at the elk. There was a bull, three cows, two calves and a couple of two year old bulls.

They choose to take the two year olds, as they were the best eating, and each would take the one on his side of the herd. Charlie settled in and took aim at his elk and, he knew, that Dick was doing the same. They had agreed that a grunt from Charlie would signal the shots and that Dick would whisper, when he was ready.

They could not get very close because the wash here was still quite close to the river and the stream was on the other side; about 500 yards away. It was a long shot, especially shooting downhill with the breeze blowing down the valley, across their shot path but Charlie knew his guns were true.

Charlie wanted the heart, this time, because it was rich meat and would be good for Ray to help her heal, so he decided for a head shot. At Dick's whisper, Charlie grunted and the two shots sounded as one. Charlie watched the remaining elk lift their heads and, with the bull trumpeting a warning, turned and ran up-river. Charlie's elk was down and not moving; shot two inches behind its eye, it died instantly.

Dick's elk was on its knees, shot through the shoulders it was suffering badly. Charlie looked at Dick and waited. He had learned that his friend was soft hearted towards animals and was not surprised when he handed him the Henry and asked, "Finish him will you Charlie?"

Taking the Henry, Charlie levered another shell into the barrel, took aim and fired, striking the elk in almost the exact same place that he had killed his elk. It dropped without a sound.

Dick was silent for a few seconds, then he said, "You're a natural dead on shot, Charlie. I don't know any other man that could make that shot twice in a row with that much accuracy and with an entirely different rifle.

A little embarrassed, Charlie said, "any one could with a little practice; come on, we've got work to do."

It only took them an hour to butcher the carcasses. They divided the load between the horses; Nails taking most of the four hundred pounds of meat and hides but they each took a quarter across their saddle horn. They had enough of a load and decided to head back to town.

About half-way back to town, they noticed a dust cloud rising from; they estimated, a fair sized group, off to the left. It was obvious after a short time that the group was heading in the same direction that they were and that they would reach the fort and town about the same time. For the next hour they watch the cloud get bigger and bigger as they drew closer together.

They were about a mile apart and a mile from town when they were able to recognize the Army patrol lead by Lieutenant Belmont, the Colonel's son. Just before the fort, the two groups passed within a few hundred yards of each other and Charlie was sure he saw Toddy's hand wave. He responded immediately with a wave of his own.

The Lieutenant did not look at them and rode on into the fort but there were hands from some of the men that waved a welcome before they too disappeared into the fort.

Charlie and Dick continued on to the Mathew's house where, after dinner, they spent the rest of the afternoon cutting, drying, cooking and smoking the elk meat. Ray and the girls helped and the time went by quickly.

They had more meat than they could eat in a reasonable amount of time, so, Charlie asked Dan if he thought that the hotel could use a half an elk. Dan called John; seems that he worked there as the house boy, doing chores, cleaning rooms and carrying luggage. "Sure could," he confirmed and agreed to help them carry it.

"Dan," Charlie asked, "would you mind if I asked John some questions about some people that we know? I won't put him on the spot, if he doesn't want to answer and the information will stay with me; I won't cause you or him any trouble."

Dan studied Charlie carefully and then replied, "Alright but I'll sit in on the talk just in case."

"Agreed," Charlie said, as they gathered on the porch. He started by telling John about Jim and Johnny and asked if there was anything strange or secretive that he saw going on.

"Well, I thought it kind of strange that Johnny went out back and spent the day with the Colonel's woman and, when she came to work tonight, she had a black eye and some bruises on her arms."

There was stunned silence for a few minutes and then Charlie asked, "What woman? Could you explain this situation for me?"

Matthew joined the group and between the two of them, they saw, heard or overheard most of what went on in town.

CHAPTER 12

A girl had come west with Arthur and she now worked at the restaurant as the waitress that had waited on Charlie and Dick. Her name was Minnie Watson, nicknamed Skinny Minnie, and she lived in a shack behind the hotel. The Belmont's took turns spending the night with her and kept her around by taking what money she earned at the restaurant. They kept her living poor and friendless so they could have her whenever they wanted to.

The Colonel had a wife back in Massachusetts that he was glad to be away from. She had caught him in a number of affairs and was taking all the money she could get away from him.

The Colonel had made advances to most of the women in town and was not well liked but, being the Colonel at the fort, he was the only law that the town had and no one dared cross him. That is no one except Tim Smith; when old Belmont made a pass at Susan, Tim's wife; it took seven men to hold Tim back from breaking him in two.

Law or no law, Tim's life revolved around his wife and son, Sam, and he allowed no one to bother them. Everyone knew that he didn't carry a gun and no one wanted to get him angry enough to fight hand-to-hand with him.

The Mathews knew him well because the Smiths were the most dedicated Christians, of the few people that came to the church and Tim was the only deacon.

Back to Arthur and Leonard Belmont; it would seem that the father and the son had the same lust problem. Arthur had come west just ahead of an angry father's shotgun. Rumor had it that he was a father three times over, by different girls and married to none of them. He also had tried to make passes at some of the local women, but did not get anywhere with any of them.

Ray was a fresh attraction for them and, being an Indian, they thought that no one would care if she ended up with them. All they had to do was get Charlie out of their way.

Charlie again felt that anger slowly burning in him against those that would take advantage of the helpless for their own gain.

The boys continued and told them that Jim just visited with his sister and their family. The rest of the time he stayed at the saloon and played cards. He spent very little time with Johnny and it was obvious that they were not on the best terms.

Johnny had spent half the night talking to the Colonel and then got in a high stakes card game. He had lost steadily and was not in a good mood when he finally went to spend the night with Minnie in her shack. He was in a better mood after he spent time with Minnie but, they think, he beat her bad; taking his anger out on her.

The sun was setting when they finished their conversation and the Mathews went to bed. Tomorrow was Sunday and they had to prepare for church.

Charlie and Dick sat for a while talking and thinking; digesting this new information. The need to go uptown and look around was gone, now. They knew what was happening and why but Charlie wanted to talk to Minnie, if he could. He suspected that Arthur would be spending the night with her tonight, where he had been away from her for so long but he thought that he would at least try and Dick thought that he could use a cup of coffee, too.

They made their way uptown warily, knowing that there were deadly elements around. Charlie remembered Dan's prediction that someone was going to die and he also remembered that he had a personal feeling about that statement. He knew that, as a Christian, he was ready to die but he couldn't help worrying about Ray and, his new found close friend, Dick. Arthur and Leonard wanted Ray and, if they got her, her life would be a living hell and Lin, alias, Johnny Gringo, had it in for Dick. Charlie believed that Dick was a brave man because he went where Charlie went and didn't seem to worry about Johnny but he also believed that Johnny was a lot faster than Dick. True, he had not seen Dick draw but he knew that Johnny was lightning fast and not afraid of Dick.

The lights were coming on throughout the town and the night saloon sounds could be heard above the movement of the people still making their way home. The store was dark along with the more earnest business' while horses lined the hitch posts in front of the saloons; many were army horses but there were quite a few from the local ranches.

They went to the hotel, first, and looked through the restaurant windows to see if Minnie was working tonight. There was a young boy serving food and cleaning up.

"I'm going to go around back and check the shack" Charlie said, "Why don't you circulate around town and see if you can locate Johnny?"

"Sure," Dick said and as he moved away, "Be careful, I have this feeling that something big is about to happen."

When Charlie reached the door of the shack, he could see a light shining under it. The windows were covered with a heavy material to keep anyone from seeing in. He knocked lightly and heard a gasp through the door. A chair fell over inside the shack and he heard a shuffling moving away from the front.

"Minnie? Miss.? I'm harmless. They call me Charlie and I would like to talk to you a little if you don't mind." Charlie heard another gasp, then a thin voice spoke, "Go…go away."

"Minnie, please. I mean you no harm." Charlie pleaded.

"I can't help you." Her voice sounded stronger and closer.

"I know. Maybe I can help you." And he heard another gasp and a fumbling at the door. It opened a crack and he saw the side of her face as she looked out. Her eye was swollen almost shut and her hair was uncombed and tangled. Anger swelled up so quickly in Charlie that he had to clinch his fists to make himself calm so he could sound casual, "I just want to talk to you for awhile. They tell me that you don't have many friends in town and I would like to invite you to visit the Mathew's sometime." It sounded lame even to Charlie but he couldn't think of anything else to say.

She opened the door a little further and Charlie saw that her clothes were in tatters. A glance behind her showed him that she lived in utter poverty. A dirty bed and bedding and a table with one chair were the only furnishings. The windows were covered with flour sacks to keep prying eyes out. Charlie's heart went out to her; she would not be much older than Ray and was living the life that the Belmont's had in mind for Ray.

"I remember you from the restaurant," she mumbled. Fear making her nervous but desperately needing someone to be her friend.

Charlie, talking low and soft, spoke of the time in the restaurant and of finding out that she was alone. He made small talk, drawing her out and relaxing her.

He knew that he was on the Belmont's territory but he couldn't abandon this hurt and abused creature.

He made small talk of her job and her home State of Massachusetts; she didn't question how he knew. Here was a gentle voice and a kind word; two things that she had desperately prayed for.

When he had her sitting on the door step and more relaxed, he gradually brought the conversation around to her condition and what caused it.

Johnny Gringo had been there all day beating and abusing her between drinks. He had left a short time ago so that Arthur Belmont could come to town and have his turn. Arthur and Leonard kept her there for their pleasure and most of the town was afraid to help. They took any money she managed to get and she had to eat the leftovers at the restaurant. The hotel owner was being paid to look the other way and she didn't know who she could trust for help, most of the town's people were afraid of Colonel Belmont and the control he had, using his soldiers to get his way.

Charlie kept his emotions in tight rein but he could feel that familiar slow-burning anger deep within.

She had been in love with Arthur in Massachusetts and had come west with him. His father had raped her on her first night here and Arthur had laughed when she told him. She had been thinking of taking a knife from the hotel kitchen and killing herself when Charlie had given her that large tip. The hotel owner did not expect her to get so much money and she was able to hang on to most of it and hide it under a rock at the corner of the shack.

All the time that they talked, Charlie knew that he would have to do something and do it tonight. Arthur was on his way and would have to be dealt with; also, Johnny Gringo [Charlie had stopped thinking of him as his old friend Lin] would have to be handled. Charlie wished that there was a lawman around to help. At least with the law to support them he would not get the government after him and be branded an outlaw.

The moon had come up and the night was almost as bright as the day. Charlie decided that he had to talk to Dan to see if he dared help with Minnie. He slipped two more double eagle coins from his hidden pocket and gave them to Minnie, "Put these with the rest for now. I'm going to the preacher and see if he will help. With the Christian folks and the church supporting you, the Belmont's wouldn't dare try anything." He said it to comfort her but he hadn't convinced himself that that was true.

She brightened and clung to his arm in a desperate act of hope. He made her understand that he would have to leave her here until he could get help and, after seeing her inside and reassuring her, he made her lock the door. Then he turned and started across the opening to the restaurant to find Dick and get some help.

He had just started when a figure, dressed all in black stepped out of the shadow of the restaurant and moved towards him. He stopped and Johnny Gringo spoke with a sneer, "So. Still the 'always-do-good' Christian are you Charlie?"

Charlie felt his stomach sink into his boots. This used to be his good friend.

"Johnny! Lin, what happened to you? You were never like this." Charlie stood with his hands spread open on both sides trying not to look like a threat as he reasoned with this man.

Johnny's laugh was a horrible thing to hear and he said, "You damn Americans; you killed my father in your damn mines and you raped and killed my mother for your fun. You wasted my sister in your whore-house and left my brothers to die tied to an ant hill." He spat. "Now you get back what you deserve."

Surprise was in Charlie's voice as he answered, "Lin. I didn't know. Don't let hate for a few poison you against us all. We're friends, remember. We taught each other; laughed and played together. Lin. I'm Chuck, remember?"

Lin's voice seemed to calm down some, "Chuck, my friend. It's been so long." He shook his head and reached out his hand as if to steady himself.

He slowly looked around at the grassy plain beside him and, turning, he looked at the town. "Where are we, Chuck?" he said in a small voice, bringing his attention back to Charlie.

Charlie sighed deep inside himself as he slowly started towards Lin. "It's OK, Lin. We're here in…"

"NO! NO!" Lin shouted as he put up his hand as if to stop Charlie "Chuck! No! You're lying. He's dead. I don't need friends; I'm Johnny Gringo and you're messing where you don't belong."

He crouched into a fighter's stance, his eyes wide and wicked as his hand started to draw for his six-gun.

As Charlie watched Johnny's hands, his brain went into an adrenalin rush; everything seemed to slow to a crawl. He had not seen such an evil look on a person's face before. Johnny was completely obsessed and was going to kill him.

He knew that Johnny was fast and a flesh wound would not stop him. Contrary to what people say, a flesh wound does not stop a person's actions. They can still aim and shoot. Charlie would have to shoot him in the head or hit a bone to stop Johnny from killing him; if he could.

Charlie's senses were on high alert and he heard the squeak of Minnie's door as it opened almost behind him. He also heard footsteps at the corner of the shack. He saw movement out of the corner of his eye, close to the town buildings.

He had heard that a person's whole life passed before their eyes, just before they died. He didn't know about that but he could sense, smell, hear, see and feel everything around him.

An owl hooted out across the plain and a night bird twittered overhead. In the street a horse stamped and blew, someone was walking on one of the porches; their boots making a hollow sound on the wood.

As Johnny's hand touched his gun, Minnie sighed and took a breath in preparation to scream. The steps beside the shack came to a halt and the shadows beside the town buildings materialized into two men. One was almost behind Johnny and the other was to Charlie's right, at the corner of the building beside the restaurant.

A piano started to play somewhere and someone started to sing a hymn. "Maybe God was opening up heaven to receive him," Charlie thought.

He saw Johnny's hand close on his gun and it started out of its holster. While Lin had taught Charlie to fight with his hands, Charlie had taught him how to handle a six-gun. Even though he could use both guns and was fastest when he did, Lin had this habit, when he was pressured and wanted to be faster, of only drawing one gun.

When you draw both guns together, a person can use the backward motion of your body to increase the speed of the draw. By only drawing one gun, a person has to twist at the waist and throw the other hand out to balance the motion; taking extra time and making the aim more difficult.

Charlie watched Johnny's gun come clear of its holster and start to lift towards him.

Charlie caught a bar of the song being sung and knew it was the hymn "Lord, I'm coming home".

Minnie started her scream and Charlie heard the click of a gun being cocked from the person behind him at the side of the shack.

It was as if Charlie was detached and just watching what was happening. He was beginning to accept the fact that he might be going home to heaven when two streaks of flame sprang out from Charlie's hands. He saw dust jump from the center of Johnny's shirt, about the middle of his breastbone. Johnny fired just as he was hit by Charlie's bullets and Charlie heard a thump and a grunt behind him. He didn't turn; he watched, in fascination, as Johnny was knocked from his feet and thrown to the ground by the heavy slugs.

He watched as Johnny's body twitched in death and a great sadness started to envelope him like a heavy dark cloud, pushing into his thoughts and numbing his brain.

He slowly turned but was in time to see another body fall away from the side of the shack with blood pumping from a wound in the middle of its chest. Dressed in a lieutenant's uniform, Charlie realized that Johnny's bullet had killed Arthur Belmont. The gun that he was going to back-shoot Charlie with hung limply in his weakening fingers as he slowly pitched headlong into the dust in the pathway from Minnie's shack.

Everything was still moving in slow motion; Minnie's scream ended abruptly when she saw Arthur fall from the side of the shack. People all over town were moving in their direction and, as the wave of sadness grew darker and colder in Charlie, he knew that he had to get away.

Dick appeared at his side and Charlie, grasping his shoulder, shook him and, pointing him toward Minnie, said, "Look out for her will you?"

Dick replied, "Sure" but Charlie was already turning away and, noticing Jim leaning over Johnny's body, walked to him and asked, "Are you going to take this up for him, Jim, or can we call this the end?"

There was a strange look on Jim's face when he turned to Charlie and said, "He was no friend of mine, Charlie. He's been looking for this for some time. He had it coming. You'll get no quarrel from me."

Without another word Charlie turned and headed straight for Dan's house. It was as if the people did not see him, they passed him on either side, hurrying to the shack; talking among themselves about what could be happening. As he got further away he met fewer and fewer people until he was alone; feet carrying him faster and faster towards the Mathew's home while his brain continued to be cold and numb.

Ray was on the porch when he walked up and, when he moved to go by the house without speaking, she spoke softly, questioningly "Charlie?"

He stopped and, in spite of his mood, was amazed at how good her English was. "Yes?" he responded, voice dull with mental pain.

"Where you go?" She did not seem to be interested in what happened; she seemed to only be interested in him. Everyone else had gone to the shack so they were alone.

"I'm going for a walk, Ray. I've got some bad thoughts in my head and a heavy heart." He sighed, "I killed a man that was once my friend." Realizing that these words were still too much for her, he had signed his answer as well.

Her sharp intake of breath was immediately replaced with, "Ray go. Ride 'Olla'." It was a statement, not a question and she rose and walked towards him.

He was about to protest but said nothing. Today was her first day to be out of her chair and walking. "Would it be fair for him to take her?" he thought but his heart betrayed him. He really liked this little girl and wanted her to come with him.

Taking her hand, he stopped her at the end of the porch, "You wait. I will get Olla." Then he hurried to the stable, calling to Joe and Olla as he went.

Joe was waiting for him at the door, just as he expected, but he was surprised to see Olla and Nails there, too.

He quickly saddled Joe and put the travois on Olla; then taking the three horses; he went back and put Ray on the travois. Putting a freshly filled canteen beside her and another on Joe's saddle horn, he filled his saddle bag with elk jerky. He threw a quick pack together and loaded it on Nails; the horses standing perfectly still, sensing that something was wrong. His rifles bristled from their scabbards ready for his immediate use.

Ray lay and watched him, not saying anything. She could see the sadness making his steps drag and his shoulders sag.

When they were ready, Charlie guiding the horses with his voice started Joe out into the plain; Ray almost beside him as Olla walked beside Joe. They looked like a group of old friends going for an evening walk as they left the town behind and wandered, it seemed, aimlessly off into the night.

Charlie's mind was still guiding his feet onto the trails that made following them hard. Subconsciously he was covering their trail; he might not want to be found later or, maybe, not at all.

CHAPTER 13

Dick had watched as Charlie talked to Jim and then start away for the Mathew's house. He noticed the sag of Charlie's shoulders and the slight sway that would take Charlie off to one side or the other as he walked.

The town's people that met Charlie and saw him, thought that he was a drunk and avoided him; allowing him to go on undisturbed.

Dick's quick glance at Jim caught him staring down at Johnny's chest and shaking his head, and then he turned and hurried to Minnie.

Coming up to her startled her but Dick quickly said, "Minnie, I'm Charlie's friend and he asked me to look after you. We have to get away from here." And, not waiting for a reply, he grasped her arm and half carried her towards a dark ally that would take them between to buildings and out to the street. She put up a little resistance at first when they had started for the darkness but had given up and was running to keep up with his longer steps when she saw that he was not stopping in the darkness.

He had immediately started looking both ways and at every person that was running to go by them to the place where the shots had been fired. Finally, seeing the one he wanted, he angled to intercept a group of people moving towards him.

He met the Mathews in the middle of the street and asked if Matthew could come with him. Looking at Dan he said, "It's urgent. I need help quick." Dan nodded his head for Matthew to go and they took Minnie into the shadow beside the store.

Looking at Matthew Dick said, "Charlie asked me to look after Minnie, here, because after that shooting she's in danger. Could we get her some clothes from the store and a hat to hide who she is?"

Matthew looked at him for a second, then at Minnie. Dick could tell he wanted to ask questions but instead he nodded and said, "I've been entrusted with a key to the store but I'll have to have the money for the clothes or they'll think that I stole them."

"Good. I'll pay for them." He said as he turned to the front door of the store.

"Charlie gave me some money and I can pay for them." Minnie spoke in a small voice as she was carried along into the store.

"Hang on to it." Dick advised, "You might need it yet."

They found a man's shirt and pants that would fit her and a man's hat and boots. Dick unwrapped them and threw them on the floor and stomped on them a couple of times trying to hide the newness of them then gave them to Minnie to put on. When she was dressed, Dick tucked her hair up and pinned it on top of her head before he put the hat on.

She looked like a boy when they were done.

By this time they could hear the Army horses racing into town and the commotion excited the town's people. Dick had told Matthew what had happened and now he said, "Best go home and stay there, Matthew; this crowd is going to get nasty and dangerous tonight and its best to stay away from them. Make sure that your family knows what to expect tonight, too."

Matthew locked the door after everything was paid for and started home saying over his shoulder, "We'll be praying for Charlie and you two."

"Thanks." Dick responded glad that at least someone besides them now knew the truth. He spied Jim talking to Todd in front of the hotel and taking Minnie's arm started for the restaurant. He still didn't know what he was going to do but hiding in a well lit place right now was better than being found and killed in the dark. He could hear the mob as the noise and excitement grew.

He had no doubt that they were looking for Charlie; guns and torches were everywhere. He just prayed that Charlie had gotten away.

He tried not to draw attention as they walked across the street and into the restaurant but he noticed that both Jim and Todd were looking at them as they entered. He led Minnie a table in the darkest corner of the room and placed her in a chair facing the room. He took a chair half facing her and half facing the room after getting a pot of hot coffee and two cups from the kitchen.

The excitement was keeping everyone outside and busy and he hoped it would stay that way.

It was not too long before the door opened and Jim appeared and, after parting company with Todd, entered the room. He didn't hesitate and after getting another cup brought a chair over and sat on the other side of the table opposite Dick, further hiding Minnie.

The two men eyed each other across the table, and then Jim said, "There's going to be hell to pay for this night, Dick. When Charlie killed Johnny, Johnny's bullet killed Arthur; old Belmont's boy."

Dick looked at him and asked, "Dead then is he? I didn't have the time to check."

"Yeh, and the Colonel swears that it was murder; ranted something about killing Arthur to cover up a triple murder that he had found out on the plains." Jim commented.

The silence grew as each pondered his own private thoughts. Minnie silently watched first one then the other from under the brim of her hat, which she had pulled down over her face in case anyone looked in through the windows and recognized her. Sooner or later Colonel Belmont would be coming to look for her and these men were her only hope.

Finally Jim spoke, almost as if he were thinking out loud, "You know, Johnny was as fast with a gun as any man I've ever seen; faster than me. If that had of been me facing him, he would be alive and I would be dead; Dick, who is this Charlie fellow anyway?" He paused and when Dick did not answer he continued, "He tried to talk him out of drawing, didn't even move until Johnny had his gun out; then drew and killed him. There's only three or four men that are that fast; John Harding, Bill Cody, Wyatt Earp, maybe, and some legend that the Indians call Talking Fire Hand. This Charlie is too young to be any of them so where did he come from and who is he?" He looked at Dick, raising one eyebrow in a questioning look.

Dick stared back, wanting to answer Jim but not knowing how far that he could trust the man. Finally he decided to take a chance and tell Jim and Minnie a little information. He started with Charlie's Christianity and personality; carefully watching their reactions so he could stop if he saw that they were too interested in the wrong things but the more he told, the more they opened up and included personal information about themselves; building Dick's trust in them.

They spent the night in the restaurant sharing information and ideas.

People looking in only saw two men and a boy in deep conversation and ignoring anyone else.

By morning they had a plan; until he caught Charlie, Colonel Belmont wouldn't be looking for Minnie so they would consult with the Mathews first. They left the restaurant together shortly after the sun came up. The town was asleep after wearing itself out during the night.

Together, the soldiers and the towns' people had searched every house, building, alley and hiding place but could not locate Charlie or Ray. The excitement causing an increase in the sale of whiskey and bullets as the mob became drunker and gunshots became more frequent. Not all of the bullets were aimed at the sky as the occasional window was shot out and bullets could be heard thumping into wooden walls. The town also lost a few of its dogs and a chicken or two as anything moving became a fleeing Charlie. Together in the dark and forced on by the ranting Colonel Belmont, the mob had a whiskey heightened courage as they boldly roamed the town all night; most of them not understanding what they were doing.

The more respectable citizens, few as they were, stayed indoors with their windows well-lit and their children against the wall that backed onto their woodsheds.

Dick, Jim and Minnie were joined by Sergeant McKinley before they reached the end of the porch. Not having the authority of his commanding officer, he had pulled as many of the soldiers that would follow him back to the stable and had protected the livestock from being shot and watching for possible fires that could be started.

After a polite 'good morning' to Minnie and a 'mornin' to Dick and Jim, he invited himself to walk along with them. After a few steps he spoke as if he were speaking to himself; "that Charlie won't be found unless he wants to be found." He paused and then continued, "He took his girl and his horses. He's got himself an arsenal with him that would stand off an army. Shore would hate to see him do something that would get him in trouble; I like that boy."

Dick had been listening but he didn't know Todd and said nothing. Then Jim spoke, "The kids think an awful lot of him too, Toddy. A man that likes kids and helps hurt people must have a few good things in him."

"You don't have to tell me that, Jim. It ain't the kids that worries me; Ruth has been on my mind all night and she swears by Charlie but she won't tell me what she knows; Just, that, if anything happens to him and I'm involved, things are going to be mighty hot for me. You know that I'm not afraid of many people in this world, Jim, but she's got me as nervous as a chicken in a fox den."

Minnie had been listening as they walked and, now, she almost wailed, "Don't let them hurt him. He's the only man that would come and help me. Please, please help him." Her chin was quivering and she looked more forlorn with her eyes wet and her mouth drawn down in anguish.

They had reached the Mathew's front porch and, as they all sat down, Jim spoke; "Easy girl. From what I've seen, Charlie is not all that easy to hurt." Turning to the sergeant he continued, "Toddy. Dick and I have been talking and I want you to hear what he has to say." And to Dick, "You can trust him, Dick. He's my brother-in-law and I'll vouch for him."

"OK." Dick said and told him what he and Jim had been talking about most of the night. As they talked, Dan and his family joined them on the porch. Everyone had spent a sleepless night watching out for each other as the town senselessly cut loose of their sanity. At one point, Dan sent Rachel to get another man that, he said, should be there and that could be trusted.

When Tim Smith and his family arrived, Dick shook his hand and told them that Tim was already one of Charlie's friends and that he should be here.

When it came time to go to church for the morning service they had all shared what was going on and had voiced their concern as to what they could do about it.

When Dan rose to go to the church, he was followed by everyone there; as if they understood that there was more to come. Dan confided that the congregation consisted of his family and the Smith's so it was a small congregation. There was adequate room for them all and lots of room left over.

Dan led in opening prayer and had picked the first hymn when there was a commotion at the door. Everyone turned to see Charlie, wheeling Ray in her chair, coming through the door.

When he had left town last night, Charlie had thoughts of not stopping but to continue on out of this country and into the next. His mind was clouded with hurt and doubt; he had KILLED his old friend.

Reason tried to tell him that he had to do it or die a needless death but his heart kept telling him that there should have been another way.

He had walked most of the night beside the travois where Ray, sensing the emotional struggle battling inside Charlie, watched silently as his face showed first one emotion and then another as the battle raged back and forth. Charlie talked; reasoning with himself about one idea and then another as he walked and the emotion kept building and building until he thought that he would explode.

Charlie had walked and fought for ten miles, twisting and turning out into the grassy plain; habits making him hide his trail so that even the best tracker would have a difficult time following them.

They had come to the crest of the valley with the stream downriver from where Dick and he had shot the elk and, in near exhaustion, he had fallen on his knees and cried out to God for understanding. His emotion had burnt him dry and he could go no further.

He had waited, head hung down; the horses standing patiently waiting also and Ray, still not saying anything, watched as Charlie waited for His God to help him.

A gentle breeze started to blow and, as Charlie lifted his head and looked out over the valley, understanding flowed into his heart, warm and soothing thought after thought made him understand that life could only exist with death. Like the elk that had to die so that those who ate them could live, evil had to die so that good people could live. The death and destruction that Lin was causing had to stop and Charlie's caring for the hurting souls had put him in the place to stop it.

Ray had watched as the mental battle stopped and relief flowed across Charlie's face as peace took over his mind. She saw that Charlie's God was very powerful and very kind and she wanted to know this God.

Exhausted but calm, Charlie had stood and walked back to Ray. He smiled at her and signed his thanks for her being there with him. Then he explained that they must go back and finish what they had started in the town. She was not as sure as he was but she had seen his strength return and signed that she would follow and trust him.

They had started back the same way they left; Charlie walking quietly beside the travois and the horses. Charlie knew, walking back to face death again.

Charlie took a seat near the back, placing Ray's chair beside his own and saying nothing. It was obvious to all present that Charlie had spent an emotional night; he looked tired and spent. Ray, even though she too was tired, had been with Charlie when he needed a friend to talk to and her pleasure at him trusting her to be there for him made her face shine, knowing that she had come through for the man she loved.

There was total silence for a while, until they saw that Charlie was not going to say anything, then, Dan, clearing his throat, again announced the hymn and they all started singing. All through the first hymn, the door kept opening and closing as the people of the town trickled in. The word had spread quickly that Charlie was back in town and was in the church. By the end of the hymn, the church was almost full of the towns' people, eager to see Charlie and see what would happen next. They sat in the pews and stood along the walls and the more timid looked in the windows and doorways; men, women and children, all curious to see this great gunslinger and to watch his destiny unfold.

By the end of the second hymn, the individual soldiers started arriving. The first man to come through the door was the Major, quickly followed by Ruth, Beth and Carl; they made their way to a place near Charlie and the Major put his hand on his shoulder to comfort him.

By the end of the singing, everyone heard the commotion outside as the main army arrived and surrounded the church, rifles ready, waiting for Colonel Belmont to arrive. Those towns' people that could not fit into the church started to ease away, trying to get out of the line of fire.

Undaunted, Dan picked up his bible and said, "I'm reading from the gospel of John, chapter three verse sixteen." Which he read and, without stopping, launched into his sermon on 'Salvation – free but what it cost'.

Charlie, watching from the back, had to admit that Dan was good. His sermon was very powerful and Charlie felt his heart jumping in tune with Dan's voice. He knew that the danger was outside but he was in God's house and what was outside God would look after.

When Dan finish, he was soaked with sweat, then, in a booming voice he cried, "It cost God the death of His Son so that you could live with Him in heaven. If you don't want to go to the devil's hell, come to this alter," as he waved his hand at the front of the church, "and repent; seek God's forgiveness and accept His gift of salvation through Jesus Christ's death on Calvary's cross and make the choice to love him. Secure for yourselves a place in His kingdom, today!" With that he stopped, waiting.

Charlie was the first one out of his seat. He didn't need to repent again but he had killed his friend, last night, and, even though he understood, he still wanted God to forgive him.

After he had talked to his God, he remembered hearing a rush of people moving to the front of the church. Looking to one side, he saw Minnie crying and praying with a mixture of town people and soldiers behind her. On his other side, Ray was quietly praying in her native Nez Pres and beyond her he thought he saw Jim.

The door of the church slammed open and Colonel Leonard Belmont stormed in, pushing his way towards Charlie. He was followed by a group of armed soldiers, eyes hard and rifles ready.

Charlie stood and turned to meet them, hands up. He had left his guns and knife on his saddle horn, knowing that he could not use them in church.

"Got you, you murdering ..." and he rambled on profanely. Then, "Sergeant, lock these two in the guard house," with his hand indicating Charlie and Ray.

The Major, standing beside Ray spoke quietly and said, "Not the girl, Colonel; she's still not well and she's under the care of the Mathew's. She won't go anywhere without Charlie so you have no reason to take her to the lock-up."

Dan had come down beside them and said, "That's right Colonel, we're looking after her and she will not be going anywhere." He stood with his feet slightly apart and firmly planted. Tim's huge shadow fell over them as he silently stepped up behind Charlie.

The room stood still, waiting as the Colonel got red in the face and looked like he would explode. His eyes bulged and his mouth opened and closed but, as he looked around, he realized that, if he pushed this about the girl right now, he would lose the support he had from even his own soldiers. He could push his command too far and he saw that the town's people were ready to rebel at the abuse that he so often used.

Growling, he push Charlie towards the door and following, pushed him a couple of more times before the door closed on them.

The room had a strange, eerie silence after they left. People started to quietly leave by ones and twos until Charlie's friends were left alone.

The Major was the first to speak, "You are all his friends?" and at their assent, he continued "Not only is the Colonel blaming Charlie for his son's death but we found three bodies out on the plain that he is claiming that Charlie murdered. The Colonel intends to find a way to hang Charlie and he has a lot of influence around here to do it." Taking a deep breath he went on, "For now, he is safe enough with Todd looking out for him. The men like Todd and he is an honest man. I don't know what the Colonel has in mind but I know it's not good. I'm going to the fort and see if I can find out anything. Ruth can bring any news you get to me and I will tell her anything that I find out so she can tell you. I guess, for now, we had better pray and pray hard, if we want to see Charlie live through this."

Outside Todd grabbed Charlie's arm and turned him towards his horses. He spoke from the corner of his mouth, not turning his head and not talking loud enough for anyone else to hear, "Relax, Charlie, and go along quietly. Remember that God is in control and your friends will support you. I'll be right here beside you to make sure no surprises happen between here and the fort."

Charlie felt himself being carried along by the soldiers. He was strangely at peace with whatever was going to happen. He had asked God's forgiveness for his having to kill Johnny Gringo and had placed the situation in God's hands. It was a strange new feeling for him to feel helpless when he had always been able to think, talk or fight his way out of almost anything.

The horses were still standing in front of the Mathew's house and the soldiers striped his weapons from them before making him mount and tying his hands to the saddle horn. As they rode to the fort, Todd stayed beside Charlie while the Colonel led the troop. He mumbled and ranted to himself as they rode, none of the men dared to approach him.

CHAPTER 14

At the fort, they put Charlie in the stockade and the Colonel posted two of his soldiers to guard him. He left strict orders to shoot Charlie, if he tried to escape, then went away mumbling something about making him an example and showing the town's people that he was no-one to trifle with.

Todd stayed behind and, taking up a chair, sat down outside the bars where he and Charlie could talk.

The building was 4 square at 12 feet long and 12 feet wide and divided in half by a barred wall. The doorway entered into the left side where there was a desk, a couple of chairs and a bench seat against the wall in the front and a small room enclosed behind the desk was small room where they kept bedding, shackles, prisoner's personal effects and buckets, pails and cleaning supplies.

The other half of the room was divided in two by a wall making up two cells with the doors opening into the room with the desk. Each cell had four single beds, bunked two on each side of the room and one over the other. Each cell had a barred window high in the center of the outside wall that shuttered from the outside in the winter to keep the cold out; they were open, now letting in the breeze and the outside noises. The prisoners washed and did their bathroom business outside of the cells. The privy was just outside a back door that was beside the little room at the back of the office.

Todd sat on a chair just outside the bars while Charlie sat on the bottom bunk in the first cell facing him. Todd told Charlie about the three dead men that the soldiers under Arthur's command had found and that the Belmont's had schemed to pin it on Charlie. The rain had washed out most of the sign and the wild animals and birds had destroyed most of their bodies but they were killed with a shotgun and a Sharps rifle; both, of which, Charlie owned.

The guards were posted outside so that they were alone and could not be heard so Charlie decided to trust Todd with the truth and told him what had happened.

After listening to Charlie's story, Todd said, "Yes, the way they were laid out would back up your story but Arthur had found a couple of friends that swore that you had murdered those men. Now, the Colonel is saying that you killed his son to keep him from arresting you and bringing you to justice. There will have to be a trial; this is the United States Army and we have laws that we have to follow."

"It was Johnny Gringo's bullet that killed Arthur, Toddy. I didn't even know that that was him beside the shack."

Just then, they were interrupted by a soldier coming in through the door. His eyes shifted nervously as he said, "Colonel wants to see you up at his office, Sarg. I'm to take over here."

There was a strange doubt in Todd's voice as he answered, "OK, Dave" then after a moment of hesitation, "Charlie hasn't eaten, yet, today, so I'll send Flapjack over with something."

The statement seemed to make the soldier more nervous and he stammered, "OK, I guess. I'll just wait in here."

Todd replied quickly, "No, send Baker in; Charlie may have to use the outhouse soon," and he looked at Charlie with an intense stare.

Catching on, Charlie affirmed, "Yes, I do; been holding it for some time now."

"Well,.....OK," and going outside they heard him call for Baker. In a moment, Baker entered the room and closed the door when Todd motioned for him to.

Todd spoke low enough so that only those in the room could hear him, "Baker, take Charlie to the outhouse and back here; then don't leave him until I return. Charlie won't try to escape and you make sure that he stays alive."

"Sure, Sarg, I wondered why Dave spent so long in the Colonel's office just to get a message for you. Man, Charlie, you know how to stir the pot, don't you? How's the kid doing?" Baker asked.

"She's healing fine, Baker. Thanks for asking." Charlie answered.

As Todd left, they went out the back door and over to the privy where Charlie done his business. They returned just as Flapjack came through the front door with a tin bucket smelling of steak and vegetables and a hot coffee pot. "Here, Baker, bring that starving low-down skunk over here so we came kill him with my awful cooking." He said with a grin and a wink.

Not to be outdone, Baker replied, "Dang right. You can feed some of that poison at supper time and get rid of a few snakes, too."

Sobering, Flapjack answered, "Easy, Baker. Snakes get theirs, too. Toddy told me to keep you company as long as I could then he's sending Bill and Dan over."

Charlie watched as his friends set up a defense around him of trusted people and quietly gave thanks to God for his help. They talked about Ray and the morning sermon's affect on the town people until Todd walked in with Bill and Dan.

They, too, asked first about Ray and her knife wound but, as the small talk died away, Charlie noticed that Todd was silent and brooding. Todd motioned him aside and, where no-one else could hear, said, "The Colonels sending me to Lewistown, in the morning, with a dispatch for the telegraph office there. It seems that there is going to be a trail tomorrow also and he intends for me to miss it."

"You have to obey orders, Toddy, and you've done a whole lot for me already." Charlie said as a way of thanking him.

"Yes, I'm a soldier and that means that I have to follow orders. The Major rode in a little while ago and is up talking to the Colonel. He might have some news for you from your friends in town." Todd's answer held hope for Charlie. He could see the elements of power struggling over control here and he began to worry for Ray.

Baker and Flapjack left with Flapjack promising to bring more of his awful cooking later; Charlie had eaten everything he had brought because he had eaten nothing since the night before.

He noticed the small scar over Bill's eye and had a twinge of guilt but soon quashed it. The cost of that scar had brought a greater good in the lives of the Indians and was worth it in Charlie's estimation.

Dan had been talking to some scouts before coming in with Todd and brought up the subject of their conversation. He said that the 'scouts were telling him that an Indian legend called 'Talking Fire Hand' was in the area and helping the Indians. As the conversation thrilled at the stories and escapades surrounding this great Indian legend, Charlie sat quietly in his cell and said very little. A couple of times he caught Todd looking at him with a thoughtful look on his face but he made himself relax and talk as if he only knew a few of the stories.

'Talking Fire Hand' was wanted by the white soldiers for questioning about a few things that he was reputed to have done and they would have liked to have got their hands on him.

The stories were well talked about when the door opened again and the Major came in. His face had a serious and thoughtful look that spelled bad news. He greeted the others and then, came over to Charlie. He told him of the group that was left at the church after the Colonel and his men had taken Charlie. The Mathews were looking after Ray and Ruth and her kids were staying to help.

By the time he was ready to head back here, to the fort, Minnie had disappeared and Dick, Jim and Tim were seen sitting in front of the stable idly passing the time.

"By the way," he added, "your presence in church, this morning, got the town and half the soldiers in to hear Dan's sermon and I counted eight town's people and three soldiers that stayed for prayer after the alter call. God does work in mysterious ways; Dan and Tim have had no success with this area for almost a year now and you show up and, …well…revival, I guess. Those people were still with Dan when I left town."

"Praise God," Charlie breathed, "But there is still something bothering you, Bob; can you tell me what it is?"

He hesitated, studying Charlie's face; then, "Charlie, the Colonel has appointed me to be the prosecutor at your trial tomorrow. It was an order from my commanding officer, leaving me no room to refuse. He's setting you up to hang and eliminating your help. He's a very cagy tactician when it comes to winning a war, Charlie."

Charlie felt the cold fingers of doubt crawling up his back again. He was still ready to die but now he would be leaving a defenseless Ray and Minnie behind and friends that had stuck with him would be persecuted and shunned; not to mention the newly saved people from this morning. Could they believe in a God that seemed to abandon His servants when they needed Him the most?

Charlie looked at his hands; turning them over he thought, "God has given me a brain to think, strength to fight and knowledge to win; maybe He wants me to break out and run away with Ray."

Todd had noticed the sudden quiet in the cell with Charlie and the Major and, as if reading Charlie's mind, came over to them and said, "Don't do it Charlie. God doesn't want people to be lawbreakers. Trust Him; He'll make a way were there doesn't seem to be a way. I don't want to have to come after you; one of us would die."

The truth shocked Charlie back to reality. Todd was right, he couldn't run. If he had to die, God would make a way for his friends. When Jesus had died on the cross, His disciples had continued and got stronger.

"Todd's right, Charlie," Major Stewart confirmed, "running doesn't solve anything and Ray can't travel that hard and recover. God will make a way; we have to have faith."

"It was easier to tell people that when I wasn't in trouble, Bob; but it sure is hard to hear it now, when I'm so worried." Charlie confided.

The Major left to go to town to tell Charlie's friends the sad news and Todd went to tend to his duties leaving Bill and Dan with strict orders to protect Charlie from any unusual death plots.

The mood in the prison seemed to get more serious and depressing as the day wore on. Even Flapjack's arrival with supper was only a brief uplift; soon replaced again with the gloom surrounding the situation.

Baker came in later to relieve Dan and said that Todd was coming in to relieve Bill. Major Bob had returned from town with Ruth and her kids. They wanted to see Charlie and cried when they were forbidden by the Colonel. Minnie was still no-where to be found and Ray would not come out of the Mathew's house.

Dick and Jim left after hearing that the trial was tomorrow and would be held in town at the restaurant. Colonel Belmont was making it a civil trial by judge alone and he, being the highest ranking officer of the United States Army in the area, would be that judge.

Charlie had to admit that the Colonel was setting this up with no hope of success for Charlie or his friends. It seemed like the Colonel had already won but his hope was still in a merciful and all-powerful God.

Would God decide to let him fall prey to the Colonel's scheme and die; like Jesus being killed by Pontius Pilate or did He have something else in mind for Charlie? Tomorrow would tell.

Charlie was awake just before sunup. It looked like an overcast day with another hint of rain. "Even the weather is gloomy," Charlie thought.

Todd had stayed most of the night but had to leave to get some sleep for the long ride to Lewistown. Baker had stayed all night. Dave had stepped in about two o'clock but when Baker had looked at him, he had said something about 'just checking' and left again.

Flapjack came in with breakfast as the sun was coming over the horizon. He told them that Todd was just leaving for Lewistown and wouldn't be back until the next day.

Major Stewart came in just as they were finishing breakfast. His news was not much better. Dick and Jim were still missing and Minnie could still not be found.

Bob had looked in on Ray but she refused to let him look at her wound and would not leave the house. Dan had tried to organize a prayer group but only he and his wife showed up.

The trial was set for two in the afternoon so that would give everyone a chance to get there from the surrounding area.

After Flapjack and the major left, Charlie spent the rest of the morning in prayer and deep thought. No answers were coming to him and all he had was to wait and hope. He knew Todd was out of it and the Major, having to act as prosecutor, could not legally help him.

Dick, Jim and Minnie were his witnesses for the shooting of Arthur and they were not around. Dan and Tim were his friends but knew nothing that would help. Ray could not understand or communication well enough in English to give a good testimony about the three ambushers and, being an Indian and with Charlie would not be believed anyways.

Charlie didn't have one thing that he could depend on right now for help except God. He didn't even know how or what answers he would give to the questions that they were going to ask. He hated lies and liars but the truth would be twisted to make him look guilty and get him hung.

Oh, he knew that Bob would accept his word but the Colonel, as the judge, would take what he wanted to hear and twist or ignore the rest. He wished that he knew a good lawyer that could help him but he didn't know any around here which means that the judge could appoint one; "Probably the town drunk," Charlie scoffed quickly losing all hope. Time was Charlie's enemy because as it dragged by his mind imagined all the worst situations possible.

Flapjack came in with the noon meal and saw how depressed Charlie was. He set the meal down in front of Charlie and, not knowing what else to do, sat down opposite him and started humming 'How great thou art'.

Charlie habitually said grace and absently started to eat. As the meal progressed, Charlie started to hum along with Flapjack and, by the end of it, was feeling much better. He started to softly sing the words that made Flapjack follow.

After the third round, he stopped and smiled at Flapjack. Sticking out his hand he said, "Thanks, Flapjack, I needed that. You lifted me up when I needed it most. I was down a long ways there."

Flapjack took his hand in a handshake and, a little embarrassed, said, "S'OK. You looked like you needed that and you've helped a lot of other people around here so, what else could I do? You just get out of this mess and look after that little girl for us."

"Your right, Flapjack, and, God willing, I will."

Dave came in just then and announced that it was time to go. He opened the cell door for Charlie and prodded him as he left his cell. Dave stopped him just before going outside and fastened a pair of handcuffs on his wrists. "So you don't get any ideas," he sneered.

Charlie's sideways glance as he went out the door showed him that Flapjack's beard stubble was bristling and his face was turning a bright shade of red but Flapjack said nothing as he glared at Dave.

The horses were waiting for them, outside, along with a dozen soldiers who Charlie didn't recognize, led by Colonel Belmont and a hatchet faced Corporal. The Colonel gave Charlie a direct look and Charlie saw a look of triumph on his face.

Major Stewart sat his horse beside Charlie's mount waiting for him. His face showed that he had got very little sleep last night.

The trip to town was made in silence and over all too soon. There was little talking as the overcast day seemed to dampen everyone's mood.

There was a crowd of town people around the restaurant when they rode up. Everyone wanted to get a look at Charlie, the condemned man. The handcuffs made a dramatic effect for the crowd and they added leg irons once Charlie was on the porch.

"Belmont was thinking of everything," Charlie thought "the handcuffs and leg irons would have everybody believing he was a dangerous criminal even before the trial."

As Charlie clumped and rattled into the restaurant, he moved slowly to his chair at a table near the front, on the left side of the room. He studied the room and the crowd looking for his friends.

Colonel Belmont had a table set up one table at the front of the room with a chair behind it for himself and another chair for witnesses halfway to the far corner and backed against the wall. There were two tables, one on each side of the room for Charlie and his representative and the other for the Major as the prosecutor. The rest of the tables and chairs were scattered over the rest of the room for the crowd. The soldiers took up guard duty along the walls and doorways with the hatchet-faced Corporal acting as the court clerk; sitting at the table beside Major Stewart with a pencil and paper.

Charlie saw none of his friends there and Ray was absent.

The crowd was still coming in, most staring wide-eyed at Charlie and his shackles, when Colonel Belmont pounded his fist on the table and spoke in a loud voice, "Settle down and be quite everyone; let's get this trial going. Major Stewart has volunteered to act as prosecutor but we need someone to lawyer for this lowlife here; do we have any volunteers?" The Major gave Colonel Belmont a sharp, hard stare but said nothing. Charlie was surprised to see so many women and children that wanted to come to such a gruesome event.

Just then, Jim walked into the room from the hotel lobby. He was dusty from head to toe and he looked like he had slept in his clothes. Even though he looked tired, he was staring intently at Charlie and seemed about ready to say or do something but was cut short by the Colonel's booming voice, "Ahh, a volunteer. Mr. Marshall, you will do nicely; you can take a seat by the accused. I'm sure, with his lack of friends, that he would welcome such a man as you to speak on his behalf."

Jim's month dropped open and he came to a full stop, surprise written all over his face.

"Come, come, Sir; we must get on with the trial," Colonel Belmont scolded. "You can catch up as we progress."

Not knowing what else to do, Jim moved to the second seat and sat down beside Charlie. The play was being staged for the crowd; with Jim caught off guard, it looked like he was reluctant to take the job. The crowd was more convinced than ever that Charlie was guilty.

Charlie also saw through the Colonel's scheming; Jim was also one of the witnesses to Arthur's death but could not testify because it would be considered bios as Charlie's lawyer. He was turning every trick he could to pull this hanging off.

"Now then, this trial can begin. Corporal Jones, call in the witnesses." Belmont motioned to the hatchet faced Corporal who went to the door and motioned to someone, in the lobby, that, by the sounds had been seated there. Two men, that were dressed like scouts, came through the door and sat down at the Major's table. They were dressed like scouts with the moccasins, buckskin pants and shirts and floppy wide brimmed hats but Charlie noticed that the clothes were too new and clean.

His eyes narrowed as he took in their too high and too new guns and holsters and new bowie knives in new scabbards. They were young men with clean shaven faces and soft looking hands and the way they walked into the room, clumping and shuffling their feet and making so much noise, would make an old Indian scout swallow his cud of chewing tobacco in disgust.

Turning to Charlie, Colonel Belmont said, "Charlie whatever your last name is; you are accused of killing three men northwest of here on the plain, in cold blood and of killing my, ah....Lieutenant Belmont and his friend, Johnny Gringo, by shooting them in cold blood in the dark of Saturday night." He paused and stared at Charlie a glint of triumph in his eye, "How do you plead?"

"Not guilty, Sir," Charlie replied calmly, without any hesitation, looking Colonel Belmont straight in the eye.

Colonel Belmont bristled that Charlie had not used 'Your Honor' as, he considered himself the judge in this court of his making; but he relented at Charlie's use of 'sir' also staring Charlie in the eyes; triumph making his mouth twitch at the corners as he fought hard not to sneer.

"Very well, then, Major; you have your instructions, proceed."

Major Stewart rose from his chair slowly and, taking a paper from his pocket, read the words to call the first "scout' as a witness.

Private Jack Stern stood and walked to the lone chair and sloughed into it; pulling his guns even higher as he tried to make them more comfortable for sitting.

It was obviously a façade that the Colonel made up and was coaching to the conclusion that he wanted. He continually corrected Major Stewart and the scout as they proceeded to bring their version of what happened out on the plain.

The scout testified that the three men were on foot, obviously because Charlie had killed one of their horses and stole the rest, and that they were walking to a rendezvous with each other when Charlie ambushed them by sneaking into the middle and shooting them down as they came towards him. They appeared to be unarmed as they could find no weapons on them and their pockets had been emptied and their belongings stolen.

Colonel Belmont's voice boomed as he said, "So, you're saying that he murdered them and robbed them, and then left their bodies out on the prairie to rot."

Stern smiled and stuck his chest out a little with pride, "Yes, Sir; that's exactly what he done." Basking in the attention he was getting.

Charlie marveled that true physical events could be twisted so bad as to convince people that they were truly evil intended.

When the Major was done reading the list of questions, he sat down; staring straight ahead of himself, pale faced and with a strained serious look.

Jim stood up and looked at Private Stern; not having heard the story of the fight he was at a loss for the truth but he tried to find some holes in the testimony. "Could you say why the three had split up in the first place, Sir?"

"Probably to be able to see more of the country and where they were going," was the man's answer.

"Probably? So you are guessing?" Jim persisted.

"What does that have to do with it?" The Colonel interrupted, "He's a scout; able to read sign and track. He can understand what happened. Go on to your next question." He scowled at Jim, not expecting or liking the questions that he asked.

"OK." Jim shrugged as he continued, "Three unarmed men moving towards one armed man intending to kill them doesn't sound quite right to me. What was their logic in doing that, Sir?"

The scout replied, "They couldn't see him; he was hidden."

Jim continued, "Did he also hide his horse on a wide open plain where one could see for miles in all directions?"

The scout started to fidget and looked uncomfortable, "He made him lie down."

"So you found the spot where his horse was made to lie down?"

"Well. Yeh. I guess." The scout stammered.

"Ah. Guessing again," Jim said holding up his hand with one finger pointed while he stood and advanced a couple of steps towards the scout in the chair.

As the Private squirmed and started looking around at the Colonel for help, the Colonel interrupted again, "If he said he did; then he did. If you have no more questions; Major; call your next witness."

Sitting down, Jim turned to Charlie and whispered, "He really means to have you hang, doesn't he?"

"Yes, he's trying it alright," agreed Charlie.

Still whispering, he said; "don't worry, your God has a plan."

On impulse, Charlie whispered, "I saw you at the alter Sunday morning. Did you make Him your God, too, Jim?"

Startled, Jim turned and looked Charlie straight in the eye, "Yes, I did Charlie. I haven't felt this peaceful before, in my life."

"Good. Praise the Lord. No matter what happens here, now, you have just made my day that much better. Thank you." Charlie turned back toward the front, his heart happy and at peace. God was working even though he did not know how or what would happen to him.

The second scout, a Private Sammy Burden, had been called and was advancing on the witness chair while they and been talking. He planted one foot on each side of the chair and was going to straddle it when his spurs got tangled in the chair legs and fell over before he could sit down. Sheepishly he turned red as he quickly righted the chair and sat down. Major Stewart reading form the paper in his hand, asked the scout to describe what they had found at the ambush site.

Having collaborated with the Colonel and the other scout, he gave the same story. Major Stewart looked paler and smaller, when he sat down again. He was obviously under a great deal of strain, knowing the truth but trying to follow his commander's orders.

Jim's turn came and he tried a different approach by asking, "How long have you been a scout for the Army, Sir?"

"We been scouting for the Colonel for six months now," he said, with pride.

"And before that, where did you work?"

"Why, we're country boys; both of us grew up with Arthur.. er, Lieutenant Belmont back in Mass. We had to track our stock, hunt and find our way through miles of forest; ain't no different there than here. Signs there for a body to read, just have to look." He said, proud in his ignorance.

"It wasn't hard at all, you say?" Jim persisted.

"Nope, sunny day and sign as plain as the nose on your face," he also was enjoying being the center of attention.

Walking towards him, Jim spoke in a controlled, stern voice, emphasizing each word with a hard step with his boots: "Even though it rained hard enough to fill footprints, straighten up downed grass and wash away most sign?"

Shrinking from Jim's approach, the scout stammered, "I...I... know what I was told. W..what I saw." He glanced nervously at Colonel Belmont.

Colonel Belmont, seeing what was happening, cut in, sharply; "stop badgering the witness. He said that he saw the sign, so, he saw the sign. I don't see any witness's for your man, so.." Just then the room fell silent as Ray walked into the room and started towards Charlie.

CHAPTER 15

S he held her head high and looked only at Charlie but her appearance and her beauty held the room silent and spellbound until she seated herself directly behind Charlie.

She was followed by the Smiths, with Minnie between them. Tim's giant form and dark scowl making the people move out of their way and giving them room to advance to their seats. The soldiers on guard along the wall looked nervously at each other and back at Tim, not liking the looks that he gave them also.

Jim hurried to Charlie, at his beckoning and Charlie quietly said to him, "She," waving to Ray "saw the fight."

Colonel Belmont saw the conversation but, before he could intervene, another commotion started at the door. This time, Ruth walked in followed by Beth, Carl and two soldiers from Todd's unit. Her eyes were cold and hard as she took a seat behind the Smiths and looked at Colonel Belmont. His eyes could not meet hers but he blustered and said, "If there is no more.."

Jim interrupted him by saying; "we have a witness to the shooting on the plain, Sir." He took Charlie's lead and did not call him 'your honor'.

"What? Who?" and, before he could finish, Jim stood up and said, "I would like to call Ray to testify." As he spoke, he walked towards Ray, holding out his hand to help her up.

Charlie signed to her that Jim was a friend and she should do as he said.

No one noticed Beth slip from her seat and pass Major Stewart a piece of paper. She quietly returned to her seat beside her mother, receiving a smile of approval from her. The Major read the paper, turned and looked at Ruth and, then, read the paper again before putting it in his pocket; his face taking on a new worried look.

Jim led Ray to the witness chair and motioned for her to sit down then, turning to the room asked, "Is there anyone here who could interpret sign language for Ray?"

The Colonel, getting over his surprise and confusion, interrupted, saying, "She's an Indian; what would she know about the truth. She's his woman and would probably lie to…" He stopped and started to rise in fear as he caught the cold hard look of death in Charlie's eyes.

Stepping between them, Jim said, "She saw the shooting and could collaborate what the scouts have said."

Colonel Belmont heard the word 'collaborate' as Jim toyed with his words and, being confused with his emotions, said, "Yeh. OK. She can agree with the scouts." Sinking back into his chair he realized too late what he had agreed to.

Ruth was already beside Ray and said, "I can read sign and interpret for her." Ray smiled at her, showing her trust for Ruth.

Jim asked her what she had seen and Ruth signed to Ray. The restaurant went silent as Ray signed and Ruth, her voice the only sound, interpreted.

Periodically Charlie noticed a movement in the ranks of the soldiers but didn't think on it much until he started to recognize more and more of them. Baker was there by the lobby door and Bill and Dan were on each side of the street door. There were about twice as many soldiers now as when they had started. The original soldiers had their rifles by their sides but the new additions only had their side arms and, Charlie noticed, they had the flaps open on their holsters.

"Strange," Charlie thought, "almost as if they were expecting trouble."

As Ray's testimony ended, Colonel Belmont, red faced and eyes bulging, leaped to his feet, shouting, "Lies, lies, all lies. This murderer killed them and my son. Everyone knew that Johnny Gringo was seen with me and he would not hurt my son. This Charlie killed him and this court has proved it. As judge, I declare him guilty and he will hang before supper." He stopped breathing hard and, in the silence, everyone heard the front door open and close again.

"No. I don't think so." Dick said. He stood just inside the door covered with dirt, looking like he had just come from a long ride. On his chest a metal badge shone, "I'm a United States Marshal and have the authority to appoint judges in a civil court," as he talked he walked into the room followed by a middle-aged man in a grey suit and Sergeant McKinley, "This is Judge James Harris from Lewistown and he has come to preside over this trial."

The surprised Colonel found his voice and called to his men, "Men, to arms! Take charge!"

Todd quickly commanded, in a booming voice; "Attention!" while he casually pointed his handgun in Corporal Smith's direction, freezing his motion to stand and draw his own gun.

The soldiers with rifles snapped to attention as was their habit, while the soldiers with side arms drew their handguns and casually pointed them at the rifled soldiers and the town's people.

Dick continued, "This trial is now in the hands of the law of the United States of America. I've deputized Jim Marshall and Tim Smith to oversee this room."

Overcoming his surprise, Colonel Belmont said, "I am the commanding officer at Fort Benton and…" Before he could finish, Major Stewart rose to his feet and spoke over him, "No, Leonard. As the fort surgeon, I'm relieving you of your command. You've been under a lot of stress lately and it is my professional opinion that it is clouding your judgment and making you unfit for command. You need to have a rest and you should take your boy back to Massachusetts and bury him."

The Colonel staggered back a step sending his chair crashing against the wall before falling over while his face turned white as realization flooded his mind.

The Major quickly moved and took his arm and started towards the door as Dick and Todd turned to their men and started orders for the room to be emptied. The situation was coming under control as both sides relaxed and order was being restored.

As the Colonel and Major passed the chairs where Minnie sat, she jumped up and screamed at him, "God have mercy on you, you…you…" She was lost for words to describe him as she stood there red faced, her mouth open and her finger pointing.

The Colonel's face went red with rage and, pushing the Major away from him with enough violence that the Major fell over a table, he lunged for her, a growl starting in his throat only to come face to face with Susan as she stepped in front of him.

Reaching for her chest to grab her and push her out of the way, he said, "Get out of my way, you cow."

Charlie watched, with amazement, the simple defense move she used. Turning her hand palm out, she slid it across her chest between his hand and her chest so, when his hand got there, she could grab three of his fingers. She turned her hand upside down and back, locking his wrist backwards and his elbow upside down. The force half turned him to his left and with a sharp downward blow, using the heal of her other hand, she broke his elbow.

The pain was so sudden and intense; he gasped and feinted; falling in a crumpled heap on the floor broken arm flopping at an unusual angle.

Looking sheepish and innocent, she said, in a small voice, "My Dad taught me that and I thought that I would never need to use it."

There was stunned silence in the room until everyone realized what had happened; then Major Stewart rose from the floor and nervously stepped forward and looked down at the Colonel. He only paused for a moment then looking up, commanded two of the waiting soldiers to get a wagon to take Colonel Belmont back to the fort.

He turned back and started to kneel and tend to the Colonel's elbow but Stopped for a brief instant and looked at Susan. Then with obvious admiration in his voice, he said, "Susan, remind me not ever to get you upset with me. His elbow is shattered and will end his military career. This may sound unprofessional but," and in a lower voice, "he did have this coming to him and I'm glad that it was a woman. His wife would thank you."

Susan stammered and started to apologize, "I'm sorry. I didn't mean to break it but I couldn't let him harm poor little Minnie."

"Don't apologize," Bob reiterated, "Someone would have had to do something like this sooner or later; he was just getting worse and was trying to take a good man's life."

The two soldiers arrived with a door and they put the Colonel on it so that they could take the Colonel to the wagon they had found.

Todd stepped up to Major Stewart and, with a sharp salute, said, "Requesting permission to stay at the trial, Sir. I read the sign at the scene of the death of those three men and I believe that I can help clear things up."

Major Stewart replied, "Permission granted, Sergeant and take those shackles off of Charlie." turning to Charlie he said, "God has come to your defense, Charlie. He's given you some good friends to stand by you."

He turned to go but stopped and half turned back again. With a twinkle in his eye, he said, "I believe that you are capable of removing Ray's stitches. They should be ready to come out now." He left with the rest of the soldiers following him.

Charlie rubbed his wrists after Todd removed the hand shackles and nodded his thanks to the grinning Sergeant and saw him wink before he turned away.

Judge Harris cleared his throat and said, "If everyone is in agreement, we can continue the trial and get this over with." At everyone's nod, he walked to the front of the room and picked up the empty chair behind the table. Ray had not moved from the witness chair and Ruth was still beside her.

Judge Harris said, "As a judge only trial, all I have to do is hear the evidence. There is no real need for lawyers." Looking at Charlie, he said, "Young man, you are the accused?" and after Charlie's "yes, Sir", he turned to Ray, "And you are the first witness to the three deaths?"

Ruth spoke for her, "Yes, Sir. She doesn't understand English very well but I understand her signs and have been translating for her." The two scouts had disappeared but no-one seemed to mind.

The judge continued, "If everyone will have a seat, we can continue, please."

Ruth signed to Ray what she had to do and she told the story again of how Charlie rode into the ambush set up by the three men and how Charlie had killed them, in self defense, and survived.

Todd took the chair next and his reading of the sign agreed with what Ray had said.

The judge pondered for a few minutes and then said, "It would appear as though it was self-defense. Would you step forward young man and......what is your name, please? I cannot keep calling you 'young man' when we are trying you."

"Charlie, Sir. Charlie Power." There was an audible gasp by the crowd in the room. A lot of the people had heard of Charlie Power, AKA, Talking Hand, the President's Indian advisor and had heard the rumors about his son, also, Charlie Power, AKA, Talking Fire Hand.

The room started to buzz with the peoples' voices all trying to speak at once. An Irish voice that Charlie recognized as Todd's could be heard over all the rest, "Talking Fire Hand! Well, I'll be da.... OW." As Ruth kicked him in the shin and gave him a sharp look to keep him from swearing in front of the children.

The judge took out his six-shooter and banged the handle on the table, "Silence, please." And looking at Charlie, "Mr. Power, I find you not guilty of murdering those three ambushers. Now, about Lieutenant Belmont; you have pleaded .....?" and he raised his eyebrows looking at Charlie.

"Not guilty, Your Honor."

"Very well; is there any witness' to the shooting?" He looked towards Dick as the representative of the law enforcement for the case.

"Yes, Your Honor." Dick said as he stood up, "this young lady, Minnie." And he waved his hand in Minnie's direction. "Jim Marshall." Pointing to Jim, "and myself."

"Good then, ladies first; Miss. would you take the witness chair and tell us what you saw, please?" The judge said. He had stood up to see and now he sat back down and calmly watched Minnie as she moved to the witness chair and sat down. Ray moved back behind Charlie, her hand brushing his shoulder as she passed.

The room had listened quietly as Ray signed and had broken into a murmuring roar until Minnie sat down. Dick brought a bible and swore Minnie to the truth, then Minnie told how she heard someone speaking and, when she opened her door, she saw Johnny Gringo drawing his gun and, then, Charlie drew and fired; hitting Johnny and knocking him down. Then she heard a noise at the side of the shack and saw Lieutenant Belmont fall to the ground.

Charlie noticed that Ruth was still interpreting for Ray; who was staring at Charlie with an approving look.

Jim was called next and his story was the same as Minnie's except he had seen Johnny fire his gun in Arthur's direction. He finished with quietly saying, "Fastest hands I've ever seen. He let Johnny pull his gun out before he started his draw and beat him; almost like he wished he didn't have to do it."

Dick's testimony was almost the same except he added that Charlie had tried to talk Johnny out of a fight before it started. Turning to Judge Harris, Dick said, "He almost had him talked out of a fight but something in Johnny seemed to snap and Charlie had no choice but to defend himself or die."

There was dead silence in the room and Charlie felt the eyes of the people staring at his back as he sat facing the judge.

The judge cleared his throat and said, "Mr. Power, I don't see any reason to go on with this trial. It was obviously self defense again. This case is dismissed."

The crowd noise started again but was drowned out by a loud whoop from Tim Smith and he was grinning from ear to ear.

Charlie didn't know what to say. As the crowd made its way out of the restaurant, he cornered Dick and demanded to know how he had arranged this.

Grinning like a kid caught with his hand in the cookie jar, he said, "It was easy; it just took a night of hard riding, a lot of organization and a whole bunch of prayer," and he explained. He was Charlie's first cousin; his father, Frank, had moved south and lost touch with Charlie and his family. When he met Charlie's dad in Washington, he had asked Dick to look Charlie up when he came west. He found Charlie's trail and had followed him to Fort Benton.

After Charlie had been taken to the fort and put in jail, Dick had told Jim and the Mathew's who and what he was but that he only had civil authority, not military. They had prayed most of the night that the Lord would make the trial a civil one. When they had learned that it was, he and Jim had ridden to Lewistown and found Judge Harris to come with them. They had met Todd on the way back and explained to him what they were doing. It was Todd's idea to send the note to Major Stewart to take command and then he brought in his own troops to help with the take over.

"You know," he said, "Belmont's career in the army is over. Susan busted his elbow good. I thought Tim would be a tough customer but I wouldn't argue with Susan, even if there was two of me. By the way, did you know who those three men were that you killed?"

Charlie looked at him for a few minutes and then said, "I found a wanted poster in their stuff and it described them exactly. They were the Nolan brothers, Jack, Doug and BJ; wanted in about three or four states, I guess.

"I think you're right and the reward on them now is a thousand dollars, dead or alive. I'll get a wire draft made up for you in the morning." Dick said.

Charlie didn't hesitate, "Make it out to Minnie, will you Dick? The poor kids got nothing and that would give her a start and a way home."

"Done!" Dick answered, the corners of his mouth turning upward, slightly, in a pleased smile.

Noticing movement at his side, Charlie turned to find Ray standing a few feet away, watching him. Holding on to each of her hands were Beth and Carl and, beside them Sam stood quietly. Beth was the first to speak, "You won!" she gushed.

Smiling at Ray, Charlie knelt down to the kids' level. "Yes, God brought me through but He said that He had some help from some kids that I knew. You wouldn't know who they are, would you Beth?"

"Oh, we prayed and prayed; mommy said that only God could help you out of this situation."

"She was right," Charlie agreed "but he used my friends to do it. That means you guys, too. He depended on you to help."

"Could you tell us some more stories, like you did in the barn at the fort?" Beth asked. "More stories." Carl echoed.

"I think I can do that." Charlie smiled, "We will have to spend a few more days here so Ray can get strong enough to travel so we can look for her people." Looking at Sam he continued, "And, I think you wanted me to show you how to shoot a rifle." He nodded and a huge smile spread across his face.

Just then, Dan walked in and came over to Charlie, "Momma and the girls have cooked up supper for you and all your friends, Charlie. After praying most of the night, she went to work preparing the food. Told the rest of us that God would do His part and we shouldn't worry about it anymore." With a twinkle in his eye, he said, "She's right again. I don't know what I would do without her."

The group started for the Mathew's house. Judge Harris proved to be a very open and friendly man and said that he felt at ease with such a fine down to earth bunch of people. Ruth and Susan took Minnie and hurried ahead to help Ann with the food and serving. Ray walked uncomfortably close to Charlie but, he told himself, she was still weak and he might have to help her.

Tim, Dick and Jim were walking behind them with Judge Harris filling him in on all the details that he had missed by not being here.

Dan, in a low voice, confided in Charlie. "At last Sunday morning's service, there were fifteen people that followed you to the front, Charlie. They gave their hearts and lives to Jesus. Jim was one and so was Minnie; God is blessing your life and will continue to use you. As you travel and have these amazing things happen to you, remember that God is in control and that He has brought the situations to you for you to act on, go through and grow," then, with that twinkle in his eye again, he added "and you will have many more exciting adventures.

A SNEAK PEEK;

Get Stone

Whity Smith stared across the room at Texas Ranger Clint Stone. He had nineteen notches on his guns and decided that this Ranger would be perfect for number twenty.

Clint had one hand on the bar and was pushing his hat back with the other while he talked to the bartender; just the edge Whity wanted. He slowly pushed his chair back as he straddled it in a crouching gunfighter's stance.

His plan was to call on him and draw at the same time to make it look like he had beaten the Ranger fairly.

Looking across the table, he caught only a hint of the shadow that disappeared under it.

Puzzled, he glanced down and froze.

Looking up at him from under the edge of the table were two pale eyes, one yellow and one green, set in the face of a huge black head; it's two inch fangs only inches from his groin and bared back from his snarling lips. His growl was only a low hiss, like a baby's soft cry, from a crushed larynx.

His pale eyes glinted demonically in the lamp light.

Whity's hands started to shake and his knees started to wobble and go weak. Everyone had heard how those fangs had ripped the throat out of the man that had killed Wolf's friend.

His face paled and his eyes bugged out as he watched those fangs move closer to his groin. He was aware of a widening wet stain that was on the front of his pants and the acid smell of warm urine filled his nostrils.

BIG EZE MOSES

Eze and Red sat their saddles looking at the cow and calf.

Eze's normally smiling face was wrinkled in a frown. He and Red had just been let go after herding cows on the bar twenty two for two years because the old man had lost so many cows to rustlers that he could not afford to keep them on.

After Red had hooked up with him, they had drifted west into the Wyoming Mountains and had found a trail that brought them to this almost isolated valley in the Hole-in-the-wall country.

They could see the length of the valley and noticed that it was surrounded by mountains with very few entrances or exits; depending on whether a cowboy wanted to get in or out.

They had started down the slope and through the rich tall grass towards the only town in the valley when they came face to face with this cow.

Eze didn't have to tell Red that this cow and calf had trouble written all over them.

They were branded with an eight triple bar connected eighty eight; a brand that would cover a lot of other brands.

That eight, eighty eight on this cow and calf covered the bar twenty two perfectly and Eze should know because he had branded this calf only three short months ago on the twenty two home range.